THE
LOST CITY

JOSEPH E. BADGER, JR.

1st WORLD
LIBRARY
Literary Society

The Lost City

Joseph E. Badger Jr

© 1st World Library – Literary Society, 2004
PO Box 2211
Fairfield, IA 52556
www.1stworldlibrary.org
First Edition

LCCN: 2005901340

Softcover ISBN: 1-4218-1155-3
Hardcover ISBN: 1-4218-1055-7
eBook ISBN: 1-4218-1255-X

Purchase *"The Lost City"*
as a traditional bound book at:
www.1stWorldLibrary.org/purchase.asp?ISBN=1-4218-1155-3

1st World Library Literary Society is a nonprofit
organization dedicated to promoting literacy by:

- Creating a free internet library accessible from any computer worldwide.
- Hosting writing competitions and offering book publishing scholarships.

Readers interested in supporting literacy
through sponsorship, donations or
membership please contact:
literacy@1stworldlibrary.org
Check us out at: www.1stworldlibrary.ORG
and start downloading free ebooks today.

The Lost City
contributed by Tim, Ed & Rodney
in support of
1st World Library Literary Society

CONTENTS.

I.   NATURE IN TRAVAIL.. 9

II.   PROFESSOR FEATHERWIT TAKING NOTES 17

III.   RIDING THE TORNADO 26

IV.   THE PROFESSOR'S LITTLE EXPERIMENT............. 34

V.   THE PROFESSOR'S UNKNOWN LAND 42

VI.   A BRACE OF UNWELCOME VISITORS................... 50

VII.   THE PROFESSOR'S GREAT ANTICIPATIONS 58

VIII.   A DUEL TO THE DEATH 67

IX.   GRAPPLING A QUEER FISH 75

X.   RESCUED AND RESCUERS 83

XI.   ANOTHER SURPRISE FOR THE PROFESSOR........ 91

XII.   THE STORY OF A BROKEN LIFE............................ 98

XIII.   THE LOST CITY OF THE AZTECS 105

XIV.   A MARVELLOUS VISION 112

XV.   ASTOUNDING, YET TRUE 119

XVI.   CAN IT BE TRUE? 126

XVII.   AN ENIGMA FOR THE BROTHERS..................... 133

XVIII.   SOMETHING LIKE A WHITE ELEPHANT.......... 140

XIX.   THE CHILDREN OF THE SUN GOD 147

XX.   THE PROFESSOR AND THE AZTEC.................... 154

XXI.   DISCUSSING WAYS AND MEANS 161

XXII.   A DARING UNDERTAKING.................................. 168

XXIII.   A FLIGHT UNDERGROUND............................... 175

XXIV.   THE SUN CHILDREN'S PERIL 182

XXV.   WALDO GOES FISHING...................................... 189

XXVI.   DOWN AMONG THE DEAD.............................. 196

XXVII.   PENETRATING GRIM SECRETS........................ 202

XXVIII. BROUGHT BEFORE THE GODS........................ 209

XXIX.   BENEATH THE SACRIFICIAL STONE................ 215

XXX.   AGAINST OVERWHELMING ODDS................... 221

XXXI.   DEFENDING THE SUN CHILDREN................... 227

XXXII.   ADIEU TO THE LOST CITY 233

CHAPTER I.

NATURE IN TRAVAIL.

"I say, professor?"

"Very well, Waldo; proceed."

"Wonder if this isn't a portion of the glorious climate, broken loose from its native California, and drifting up this way on a lark?"

"If so, said lark must be roasted to a turn," declared the third (and last) member of that little party, drawing a curved fore-finger across his forehead, then flirting aside sundry drops of moisture. "I can't recall such another muggy afternoon, and if we were only back in what the scientists term the cyclone belt -"

"We would be all at sea," quickly interposed the professor, the fingers of one hand vigorously stirring his gray pompadour, while the other was lifted in a deprecatory manner. "At sea, literally as well as metaphorically, my dear Bruno; for, correctly speaking, the ocean alone can give birth to the cyclone."

"Why can't you remember anything, boy?" sternly cut in the roguish-eyed youngster, with admonitory forefinger, coming to the front. "How many times have I told you never to say blue when you mean green? Why don't you say Kansas zephyr? Or windy-auger? Or twister? Or whirly-gust on a corkscrew wiggle-waggle? Or - well, almost any other old thing that you can't think of at the right time? W-h-e-w! Who mentioned sitting on a snowdrift, and sucking at an icicle? Hot? Well, now, if this isn't a genuine old cyclone breeder, then I wouldn't ask a cent!"

Waldo Gillespie let his feet slip from beneath him, sitting down with greater force than grace, back supported against a gnarled juniper, loosening the clothes at his neck while using his other hand to ply his crumpled hat as a fan.

Bruno laughed outright at this characteristic anticlimax, while Professor Featherwit was obliged to smile, even while compelled to correct.

"Tornado, please, nephew; not cyclone."

"Well, uncle Phaeton, have it your own way. Under either name, I fancy the thing-a-ma-jig would kick up a high old bobbery with a man's political economy should it chance to go bu'st right there!

And, besides, when I was a weenty little fellow I was taught never to call a man a fool or a liar -"

"Waldo!" sharply warned his brother, turning again.

"So long as I knew myself to be in the wrong," coolly finished the youngster, face grave, but eyes twinkling, as they turned towards his mistaken mentor. "What is it, my dear Bruno?"

"There is one thing neither cyclone nor tornado could ever deprive you of, Kid, and that is -"

"My beauty, wit, and good sense, - thanks, awfully! Nor you, my dear Bruno, although my inbred politeness forbids my explaining just why."

There was a queer-sounding chuckle as Professor Featherwit

JOSEPH E. BADGER, JR.

turned away, busying himself about that rude-built shed and shanty which sheltered the pride of his brain and the pet of his heart, while Bruno smiled indulgently as he took a few steps away from those stunted trees in order to gain a fairer view of the stormy heavens.

Far away towards the northeast, rising above the distant hill, now showed an ugly-looking cloud-bank which almost certainly portended a storm of no ordinary dimensions.

Had it first appeared in the opposite quarter of the horizon, Bruno would have felt a stronger interest in the clouds, knowing as he did that the miscalled "cyclone" almost invariably finds birth in the southwest. Then, too, nearly all the other symptoms were noticeable, - the close, "muggy" atmosphere; the deathlike stillness; the lack of oxygen in the air, causing one to breathe more rapidly, yet with far less satisfying results than usual.

Even as Bruno gazed, those heavy cloud-banks changed, both in shape and in colour, taking on a peculiar greenish lustre which only too accurately forebodes hail of no ordinary force.

His cry to this effect brought the professor forth from the shed-like shanty, while Waldo roused up sufficiently to speak:

"To say nothing of yonder formation way out over the salty drink, my worthy friends, who intimated that a cyclone was born at sea?"

Professor Featherwit frowned a bit as his keen little rat-like eyes turned towards that quarter of the heavens; but the frown was not for Waldo, nor for his slightly irreverent speech.

Where but a few minutes before there had been only a few light clouds in sight, was now a heavy bank of remarkable shape, its crest a straight line as though marked by an enormous ruler, while the lower edge was broken into sharp points and irregular sections, the whole seeming to float upon a low sea of grayish copper.

"Well, well, that looks ugly, decidedly ugly, I must confess," the wiry little professor spoke, after that keen scrutiny.

"Really, now?" drawled Waldo, who was nothing if not contrary on the surface. "Barring a certain little topsy-turvyness which is something out of the ordinary, I'd call that a charming bit of - Great guns and little cannon-balls!"

For just then there came a shrieking blast of wind from out the northeast, bringing upon its wings a brief shower of hail, intermingled with great drops of rain which pelted all things with scarcely less force than did those frozen particles.

"Hurrah!" shrilly screamed Waldo, as he dashed out into the storm, fairly revelling in the sudden change. "Who says this isn't 'way up in G?' Who says - out of the way, Bruno! Shut that trap-door in your face, so another fellow may get at least a share of the good things coming straight down from - ow - wow!"

Through the now driving rain came flashing larger particles, and one of more than ordinary size rebounded from that curly pate, sending its owner hurriedly to shelter beneath the scrubby trees, one hand ruefully rubbing the injured part.

Faster fell the drops, both of rain and of ice, clattering against the shanty and its adjoining shed with an uproar audible even above the sullenly rolling peals of heavy thunder.

The rain descended in perfect sheets for a few minutes, while the hailstones fell thicker and faster, growing in size as the storm raged, already beginning to lend those red sands a pearly tinge with their dancing particles. Now and then an aerial monster would fall, to draw a wondering cry from the brothers, and on more than one occasion Waldo risked a cracked crown by dashing forth from shelter to snatch up a remarkable specimen.

"Talk about your California fruit! what's the matter with good old Washington Territory?" he cried, tightly clenching one fist and holding a hailstone alongside by way of comparison. "Look at that, will you? Isn't it a beauty? See the different shaded rings of white and clear ice. See - brother, it is as large as my fist!"

But for once Professor Phaeton Featherwit was fairly deaf to the claims of this, in some respects his favourite nephew, having scuttled back beneath the shed, where he was busily stowing away sundry articles of importance into a queerly shaped machine which those rough planks fairly shielded from the driving storm.

Having performed this duty to his own satisfaction, the professor came back to where the brothers were standing, viewing with them such of the storm as could be itemised. That was but little, thanks to the driving rain, which cut one's vision short at but a few rods, while the deafening peals of thunder prevented any connected conversation during those first few minutes.

"Good thing we've got a shelter!" cried Waldo, involuntarily shrinking as the plank roof was hammered by several mammoth stones of ice. "One of those chunks of ice would crack a fellow's skull just as easy!"

Yet the next instant he was out in the driving storm, eagerly snatching at a brace of those frozen marvels, heedless of his own risk or of the warning shouts sent after him by those cooler-brained comrades.

Thunder crashed in wildest unison with almost blinding sheets of lightning, the rain and hail falling thicker and heavier than ever for a few moments; but then, as suddenly as it had come, the storm passed on, leaving but a few scattered drops to fetch up the rear.

"Isn't that pretty nearly what people call a cloudburst, uncle

Phaeton?" asked Bruno, curiously watching that receding mass of what from their present standpoint looked like vapour.

"Those wholly ignorant of meteorological phenomena might so pronounce, perhaps, but never one who has given the matter either thought or study," promptly responded the professor, in no wise loth to give a free lecture, no matter how brief it might be, perforce. "It is merely nature seeking to restore a disturbed equilibrium; a current of colder air, in search of a temporary vacuum, caused by -"

"But isn't that just what produces cy - tornadoes, though?" interrupted Waldo, with scant politeness.

"Precisely, my dear boy," blandly agreed their mentor, rubbing his hands briskly, while peering through rain-dampened glasses, after that departing storm. "And I have scarcely a doubt but that a tornado of no ordinary magnitude will be the final outcome of this remarkable display. For, as the record will amply prove, the most destructive windstorms are invariably heralded by a fall of hail, heavy in proportion to the -"

"Then I'd rather be excused, thank you, sir!" again interrupted the younger of the brothers, shrugging his shoulders as he stepped forth from shelter to win a fairer view of the space stretching away towards the south and the west. "I always laughed at tales of hailstones large as hen's eggs, but now I know better. If I was a hen, and had to match such a pattern as these, I'd petition the legislature to change my name to that of ostrich, - I just would, now!"

Bruno proved to be a little more amenable to the law of politeness, and to him Professor Featherwit confined his sapient remarks for the time being, giving no slight amount of valuable information anent these strange phenomena of nature in travail.

He spoke of the different varieties of land-storms, showing how a tornado varied from a hurricane or a gale, then again

JOSEPH E. BADGER, JR.

brought to the front the vital difference between a cyclone, as such, and the miscalled "twister," which has wrought such dire destruction throughout a large portion of our own land during more recent years.

While that little lecture would make interesting reading for those who take an interest in such matters, it need scarcely be reproduced in this connection, more particularly as, just when the professor was getting fairly warmed up to his work, an interruption came in the shape of a sharp, eager shout from the lips of Waldo Gillespie.

"Look - look yonder! What a funny looking cloud that is!"

A small clump of trees growing upon a rising bit of ground interfered with the view of his brother and uncle, for Waldo was pointing almost due southeast; yet his excitement was so pronounced that both the professor and Bruno hastened in that direction, stopping short as they caught a fair sight of the object indicated.

A mighty mass of wildly disturbed clouds, black and green and white and yellow all blending together and constantly shifting positions, out of which was suddenly formed a still more ominous shape.

A mass of lurid vapour shot downwards, taking on the general semblance of a balloon, as it swayed madly back and forth, an elongating trunk or tongue reaching still nearer the earth, with fierce gyrations, as though seeking to fasten upon some support.

Not one of that trio had ever before gazed upon just such another creation, yet one and all recognised the truth, - this was a veritable tornado, just such as they had read in awed wonder about, time and time again.

Neither one of the brothers Gillespie were cravens, in any sense of the word, but now their cheeks grew paler, and they seemed to shrink from yonder airy monster, even while watching it grow into shape and awful power.

Professor Featherwit was no less absorbed in this wondrous spectacle, but his was the interest of a scientist, and his pulse beat as ordinary, his brain remaining as clear and calm as ever.

"I hardly believe we have anything to fear from this tornado, my lads," he said, taking note of their uneasiness. "According to both rule and precedent, yonder tornado will pass to the east of our present position, and we will be as safe right here as though we were a thousand miles away."

"But, - do they always move towards the northeast, uncle Phaeton?"

"As a rule, yes; but there are exceptions, of course. And unless this should prove to be one of those rare ex - er -"

"Look!" cried Waldo, with swift gesticulation. "It's coming this way, or I never - ISN'T it coming this way?"

"Unless this should prove to be one of those rare exceptions, my dear boy, I can promise you that - Upon my soul!" with an abrupt change of both tone and manner, "I really believe it IS coming this way!"

"It is - it is coming! Get a move on, or we'll never know - hunt a hole and pull it in after you!" fairly screamed Waldo, turning in flight.

JOSEPH E. BADGER, JR.

CHAPTER II.

PROFESSOR FEATHERWIT TAKING NOTES.

"To the house!" cried the professor, raising his voice to over-come yonder sullen roar, which was now beginning to come their way. "Trust all to the aeromotor, and 'twill be well with us!"

The wiry little man of science himself fell to work with an energy which told how serious he regarded the emergency, and, acting under his lead, the brothers manfully played their part.

Just as had been done many times before this day, a queer-looking machine was shoved out from the shed, gliding along the wooden ways prepared for that express purpose, while Professor Featherwit hurried aboard a few articles which past experience warned him might prove of service in the hours to come, then sharply cried to his nephews:

"Get aboard, lads! Time enough, yet none to spare in idle motions. See! The storm is drifting our way in deadly earnest!"

And so it seemed, in good sooth.

Now fairly at its dread work of destruction, tearing up the rain dampened dirt and playing with mighty boulders, tossing them here and there, as a giant of olden tales might play with jackstones, snapping off sturdy trees and whipping them to splinters even while hurling them as a farmer sows his grain.

Just the one brief look at that aerial monster, then both lads hung fast to the hand-rail of rope, while the professor put that cunning machinery in motion, causing the air-ship to rise from its ways with a sudden swooping movement, then soaring upward and onward, in a fair curve, as graceful and steady as a bird on wing.

All this took some little time, even while the trio were working as men only can when dear life is at stake; but the flying-machine was afloat and fairly off upon the most marvellous journey mortals ever accomplished, and that ere yonder death-balloon could cover half the distance between.

"Grand! Glorious! Magnificent!" fairly exploded the professor, when he could risk a more comprehensive look, right hand tightly gripping the polished lever through which he controlled that admirable mechanism. "I have longed for just such an opportunity, and now - the camera, Bruno! We must never neglect to improve such a marvellous chance for - get out the camera, lad!"

"Get out of the road, rather!" bluntly shouted Waldo, face unusually pale, as he stared at yonder awful force in action. "Of course I'm not scared, or anything like that, uncle Phaeton, but - I want to rack out o' this just about the quickest the law allows! Yes, I DO, now!"

"Wonderful! Marvellous! Incredible! That rara avis, an exception to all exceptions!" declared the professor, more deeply stirred than either of his nephews had ever seen him before. "A genuine tornado which has no eastern drift; which heads as directly as possible towards the northwest, and at the same time - incredible!"

Only ears of his own caught these sentences in their entirety, for now the storm was fairly bellowing in its might, formed of a variety of sounds which baffles all description, but which, in itself, was more than sufficient to chill the blood of even a brave man. Yet, almost as though magnetised by that frightful force, the professor was holding his air-ship steady, loitering there in its direct path, rather than fleeing from what surely would prove utter destruction to man and machine alike.

For a few moments Bruno withstood the temptation, but then leaned far enough to grasp both hand and tiller, forcing them in the requisite direction, causing the aeromotor to swing easily around and dart away almost at right angles to the track of the tornado.

That roar was now as of a thousand heavily laden trains rumbling over hollow bridges, and the professor could only nod his approval when thus aroused from the dangerous fascination. Another minute, and the air-ship was floating towards the rear of the balloon-shaped cloud itself, each second granting the passengers a varying view of the wonder.

True to the firm hand which set its machinery in motion, the flying-machine maintained that gentle curve until it swung around well to the rear of the cloud, where again Professor Featherwit broke out in ecstatic praises of their marvellous good fortune.

" 'Tis worth a life's ransom, for never until now hath mortal being been blessed with such a magnificent opportunity for taking notes and drawing deductions which -"

The professor nimbly ducked his head to dodge a ragged splinter of freshly torn wood which came whistling past, cast far away from the tornado proper by those erratic winds. And at the same instant the machine itself recoiled, shivering and creaking in all its cunning joints under a gust of wind which seemed composed of both ice and fire.

"Oh, I say!" gasped Waldo, when he could rally from the sudden blow. "Turn the old thing the other way, uncle Phaeton, and let's go look for - well, almost anything's better than this old cyclone!"

"Tornado, lad," swiftly corrected the man of precision, leaning far forward, and gazing enthralled upon the vision which fairly thrilled his heart to its very centre. "Never again may we have such another opportunity for making - "

They were now directly in the rear of the storm, and as the air-ship headed across that track of destruction, it gave a drunken stagger, casting down its inmates, from whose parching lips burst cries of varying import.

"Air! I'm choking!" gasped Bruno, tearing open his shirt-collar with a spasmodic motion.

"Hold me fast!" echoed Waldo, clinging desperately to the life-line. "It's drawing me - into the - ah!"

Even the professor gave certain symptoms of alarm for that moment, but then the danger seemed past as the ship darted fairly across the storm-trail, hovering to the east of that aerial phantom.

There was no difficulty in filling their lungs now, and once more Professor Featherwit headed the flying-machine directly for the balloon-shaped cloud, modulating its pace so as to maintain their relative position fairly well.

"Take note how it progresses, - by fits and starts, as it were," observed Featherwit, now in his glory, eyes asparkle and muscles aquiver, hair bristling as though full of electricity, face glowing with almost painful interest, as those shifting scenes were for ever imprinted upon his brain.

"Sort of a hop, step, and jump, and that's a fact," agreed Waldo, now a bit more at his ease since that awful sense of suffocation was lacking. "I thought all cyclones -"

"Tornado, my DEAR boy!" expostulated the professor.

"I thought they all went in holy hurry, like they were sent for and had mighty little time in which to get there. But this one, - see how it stops to dance a jig and bore holes in the earth!"

"Another exception to the general rule, which is as you say," admitted the professor. "Different tornadoes have been timed as moving from twelve to seventy miles an hour, one passing a given point in half a score of seconds, at another time being registered as fully half an hour in clearing a single section.

"Take the destructive storm at Mount Carmel, Illinois, in June of '77. That made progress at the rate of thirty-four miles an hour, yet its force was so mighty that it tore away the spire, vane, and heavy gilded ball of the Methodist church, and kept it in air over a distance of fifteen miles.

"Still later was the Texas tornado, doing its awful work at the rate of more than sixty miles an hour; while that which swept through Frankfort, Kansas, on May 17, 1896, was fully a half-hour in crossing a half-mile stretch of bottom-land adjoining the Vermillion River, pausing in its dizzy waltz upon a single spot for long minutes at a time."

"Couldn't have been much left when it got through dancing, if that storm was anything like this one," declared Waldo, shivering a bit as he watched the awful destruction being wrought right before their fascinated eyes.

Trees were twisted off and doubled up like blades of dry grass. Mighty rocks were torn apart from the rugged hills, and huge boulders were tossed into air as though composed of paper. And over all ascended the horrid roar of ruin beyond description, while from that misshapen balloon-cloud, with its flattened top, the electric fluid shone and flashed, now in great sheets as of flame, then in vicious spurts and darts as though innumerable snakes of fire had been turned loose by the winds.

Still the aerial demon bored its almost sluggish course straight towards the northwest, in this, as in all else, seemingly bent on proving itself the exception to all exceptions as Professor Featherwit declared.

The savant himself was now in his glory, holding the tiller between arm and side, the better to manipulate his hand-camera, with which he was taking repeated snap-shots for future development and reference.

Truly, as he more than once declared, mortal man never had, nor mortal man ever would have, such a glorious opportunity for recording the varying phases of nature in travail as was now vouchsafed themselves.

"Just think of it, lads!" he cried, almost beside himself with enthusiasm. "This alone will be sufficient to carry our names ringing through all time down the corridors of undying fame! This alone would be more than enough to - Look pleasant, please!"

In spite of that awful vision so perilously close before them, and the natural uncertainty which attended such a reckless venture, Waldo could not repress a chuckle at that comical conclusion, so frequently used towards himself when their uncle was coaxing them to pose before his pet camera.

"Is it - surely this is not safe, uncle Phaeton?" ventured Bruno, as another retrograde gust of air smote their apparently frail conveyance with sudden force.

"Let's call it a day's work, and knock off," chimed in Waldo. "If the blamed thing should take a notion to balk, and rear back on its haunches, where'd we come out at?"

Professor Featherwit made an impatient gesture by way of answer. Speech just then would have been worse than useless, for that tremendous roaring, crashing, thundering of all sounds, seemed to fall back and envelop the air-ship as with a pall.

A shower of sand and fine debris poured over and around them, filling ears and mouths, and blinding eyes for the moment, forcing the brothers closer to the floor of the aerostat, and even compelling the eager professor to remit his taking of notes for future generations.

Then, thin and reed-like, yet serving to pierce that temporary obscurity and horrible jangle of outer sounds, came the voice of their relative:

"Fear not, my children! The Lord is our shield, and so long as he willeth, just so long shall we - Ha! didn't I tell ye so?"

For the blinding veil was torn away, and once again the trio of adventurers might watch yonder grandly awesome march of devastation.

"Heading direct for the Olympics!" declared Professor Feather-wit, digging the sand out of his eyes and striving to clean his glasses without removing them, clinging to tiller and camera through all. "What a grand and glorious guide 'twould be for us!"

"If we could only hitch on - like a tin can to the tail of a dog!" suggested Waldo, with boyish sarcasm. "Not any of that in mine, thank you! I can wait. No such mighty rush. No, - SIR!"

There came no answer to his words, for just then that swooping air-demon turned to vivid fire, lightning playing back and forth, from side to side, in every conceivable direction, until in spite of the broad daylight its glory pained those watching eyes.

"Did you ever witness the like!" awesomely cried Bruno, gazing like one fascinated. "Who could or would ever believe all that, even if tongue were able to portray its wondrous beauty?"

"What a place that would be for popping corn!" contributed

Waldo, practical or nothing, even under such peculiar circumstances. "If I had to play poppy, though, I'd want a precious long handle to the concern!"

More intensely interested than ever, Professor Featherwit plied his shutter, taking shot after shot at yonder aerial phenomena, feeling that future generations would surely rise up to call him blessed when the results of his experiments were once fairly spread before the world.

And hence it came to pass that still more thrilling experiences came unto these daring navigators of space, and that almost before one or the other of them could fairly realise that greater danger really menaced both their air-ship and their lives.

Another whirly-gust of sand and other debris assailed the flying-machine, and while sight was thus rendered almost useless for the time being, the aerostat began to sway and reel from side to side, shivering as though caught by an irresistible power, yet against which it battled as though instinct with life and brain-power.

Once again the adventurers found it difficult to breathe, while an unseen power seemed pressing them to that floor as though - Thank heaven!

Just as before, that cloud was swept away, and again air came to fill those painfully oppressed lungs. Once again the trio cleared their eyes and stared about, only to utter simultaneous cries of alarm.

For, brief though that period of blindness had been, 'twas amply sufficient to carry the aeromotor perilously near yonder storm-centre, and though Professor Featherwit gripped hard his tiller, trying all he knew to turn the air-ship for a safer quarter,-'twas all in vain!

"Haste, - make haste, uncle Phaeton!" hoarsely panted Bruno, leaning to aid the professor. "We will be sucked in and - hasten, for life!"

"I can't, - we're already - in the - suction!"

CHAPTER III.

RIDING THE TORNADO.

Whether it was that the air-ship itself had increased its speed during those few moments of dense obscurity, or whether the madly whirling winds had taken a retrograde movement at that precise time, could only be a matter of conjecture; but the ominous fact remained.

The aerostat was fairly over the danger-line, and, despite all efforts being made to the contrary, was being drawn directly towards that howling, crashing, thundering mass of destructive energy.

Already the inmates felt themselves being sucked from the flying-machine, and instinctively tightened their grip upon hand-rail and floor, gasping and oppressed, breath failing, and ribs apparently being crushed in by that horrible pressure.

"Hold fast - for life!" pantingly screamed Professor Featherwit, as he strove in vain to check or change the course of his aero-motor, now for the first time beyond control of that master-hand.

A few seconds of soul-trying suspense, during which the flying-machine shivered from stem to stern, almost like a human creature in its death-agony, creaking and groaning, with shrill sounds coming from those expanded, curved wings, as the suction increased; then -

A merciful darkness fell over those sorely imperilled beings, and the vessel itself seemed about to be overwhelmed by an avalanche of sand and dirt and mixed debris. Then came a dizzy, rocking lurch, followed by a shock which nearly cast uncle and nephews from their frantic holds, and the air-ship appeared to be whirled end for end, cast hither and yon, wrenched and twisted as though all must go to ruin together.

A blast as of superheated air smote upon them one moment, while in the next they were whirled through an icy atmosphere, then tossed dizzily to and fro, as their too-frail vehicle spun upward as though on a journey to the far-away stars.

A shrieking blast of wind served to briefly clear away the choking dust, affording the trio a fleeting glimpse of their immediate surroundings: hurtling sticks and stones, splintered tops of trees, shrubs with wildly lashing roots freshly torn from the bed of years, all madly spinning through a blinding, scorching, freezing mass of crazily battling winds, the different currents twining and weaving in and out, as so many hideous serpents at play.

A moment thus, then that horrid uproar grew still more deafening, and the air-ship was whirled high and higher, in a dizzy dance, those luckless creatures clinging fast to whatever their frenzied hands might clutch, feeling that this was the end of all.

Further sight was denied them. They were powerless to move a limb, save as jerked painfully by those shrieking currents. Breath was taken away, and an enormous weight bore down upon them, threatening to produce a fatal collapse through their ribs giving way.

Upward whirled the flying-machine, powerless now as those wretched beings within its cunning shape, smitten sharply here and there by some of those ascending missiles, yet without receiving material injury; until a last shivering lurch came, ending in a sudden fall.

A dizzying swoop downward, but not to death and destruction, for the aerostat alighted easily upon what appeared to
be a sort of air-cushion, and, though unsteady for a brief space,
then settled upon an even keel.

"Cling fast - for life!" huskily gasped the professor, unwittingly
repeating the caution which had last crossed his lips, which he
had ever since been striving to enunciate, faithful to his
guardianship over these, his sole surviving relatives.

"I don't - where are we?"

Waldo lifted his head to peer with half-blind eyes about them,
in which action he was imitated by both brother and uncle;
but, for a brief space, they were none the wiser.

All around the aeromotor rose a wall of whirling winds,
seemingly impenetrable, apparently within reach of an
extended arm, changing colour with each fraction of a second,
hideously beautiful, yet never twice the same in blend or
mixture.

A hollow, strangely sounding roar was perceptible; one instant
coming as from the far distance, then from nigh at hand,
causing the air-ship to quiver and tremble, as a sentient being
might in the presence of a torturing death.

"Look - upward!" panted Bruno, a few seconds later, his face as
pale as that of a corpse, in spite of the dirt and blotches of
sticky mud with which he had been peppered during that dizzy
whirl.

Mechanically his companions in peril obeyed, catching breath
sharply, as they saw a clear sky and yellow sunshine far above, -
so awfully far they were, that it seemed like looking upward
from the bottom of an enormously deep well.

JOSEPH E. BADGER, JR.

And then the marvellous truth flashed upon the brain of Phaeton Featherwit, almost robbing him of all power of speech. Still he managed to jerkily ejaculate:

"We're inside, - riding the - tornado - itself!"

Then those whirling winds closed quickly above them, shutting out the sunlight, hiding the heavens from their view, enclosing that vehicle and its occupants, as they were borne away into unknown regions, within the very heart of the tornado itself!

Yet, incredible as it surely seems, no actual harm came to the trio or to their flying-machine as it swayed gently upon its airy cushion, although from every side came the horrid roar of destruction, while ever and anon they could glimpse a wrestling tree or torn mass of shrubbery whizzing upward and outward, to be flung far away beyond the vortex of electrical winds.

Once more came that awful sense of suffocation. That painted pall closed down upon them, robbing their lungs of air, one instant fairly crisping their hair with a touch of fire, only to send an icy chill to their veins a moment later.

In vain they struggled, fighting for breath, as a fish gasps when swung from its native element. While that horrid pressure endured, man, youth, and boy alike were powerless.

Again the pall lifted, folding back and blending with those madly circling currents, once again affording a glimpse of yonder far-away heavens, so marvellously clear, and bright, and peaceful in seeming!

Weakened by those terrible moments, Bruno and Waldo lay gasping, trembling, faint of heart and ill of body, yet filling their lungs with comparatively pure air, - pity there was so little of it to win!

Professor Featherwit still had thought and care for his nephews rather than himself alone, and pantingly spoke, as he dragged himself to the snug locker, where many important articles had been stowed away:

"Here - suck life - compressed air!"

With husky cries the brothers caught at the tubes offered, the method of working which had so often been explained by their relative.

Once more the tube became a chamber, and that horrid force threatened to flatten their bodies; but the worst had passed, for that precious cylinder now gave them air to inhale, and they were enabled to wait for the lifting of the cloud once more.

Thanks to this important agency, strength and energy both of body and of mind now came back to the air-voyagers, and after a little they could lift their heads to peer around them with growing wonder and curiosity.

There was little room left for doubting the wondrous truth, and yet belief was past their powers during those first few minutes.

All around them whirled and sped those maddened winds, curling and twisting, rising and falling, mixing in and out as though some unknown power might be weaving the web of destiny.

Now dull, now brilliant, never twice the same, but ever changing in colour as in shape, while stripes and zigzags of lightning played here and there with terrifying menace, those walls of wind held an awfully fascinating power for uncle and nephews.

From every side came deadened sounds which could bear but a single interpretation: the tornado was still in rapid motion, was still tearing and rending, crushing and battering, leaving dire destruction and ruin to mark its advance, and these were the sounds that recorded its ugly work.

In goodly measure revived by the compressed air, which was regulated in flow to suit his requirements by a device of his own, Professor Featherwit now looked around with something of his wonted animation, heedless of his own peril for the moment, so great was his interest in this marvellous happening.

So utterly incredible was it all that, during those first few minutes of rallying powers, he dared not express the belief which was shaping itself, gazing around in quest of still further confirmation.

He took note of the windy walls about their vessel, rising upward for many yards, irregular in shape and curvature here and there, but retaining the general semblance of a tube with flaring top. He peered over the edge of the basket, to draw back dizzily as he saw naught but yeasty, boiling, seething clouds below, - a veritable air-cushion which had served to save the pet of his brain from utter destruction at the time of falling within -

Yes, there was no longer room for doubt, - they were actually inside the distorted balloon, so dreaded by all residents of the tornado belt!

"What is it, uncle?" huskily asked Bruno, likewise rallying under that beneficial influence. "Where are we now?"

"Where I'm wishing mighty hard we wasn't, anyhow!" contributed Waldo, with something of his usual energy, although, judging from his face and eyes, the youngster had suffered more severely than either of his comrades in peril.

Professor Featherwit broke into a queerly sounding laugh, as he waved his free hand in exultation before speaking:

"Where no living being ever was before us, my lads, - riding the tornado like a - ugh!"

The air-ship gave an awkward lurch just then, and down went the little professor to thump his head heavily against one corner of the locker. Swaying drunkenly from side to side, then tossing up and down, turning in unison with those fiercely whirling clouds, the aeromotor seemed at the point of wreck and ruin.

Desperately the trio clung to the life-lines, clenching teeth upon the life-giving tubes as that terrible pressure increased so much that it seemed impossible for the human frame to longer resist.

Fortunately that ordeal did not long endure, and again relief came to those so sorely oppressed. A brief gasping, sighing, stretching as the aerostat resumed its level position, merely rocking easily within that partial vacuum, and then Waldo huskily suggested:

"Looks like the blame thing was sick at the stomach!"

No doubt this was meant for a feeble attempt at joking, but Professor Featherwit took it for earnest, and made quick reply:

"That is precisely the case, my dear lad, and I am greatly joyed to find that you are not so badly frightened but that you can assist me in taking notes of this wondrous happening. To think that we are the ones selected for -"

"I say, uncle Phaeton."

"Well, my lad?"

"If this thing is really sick at the stomach, when will it erupt? I'd give a dollar and a half to just get out o' this, science or no science, notes or no notes at all!"

"Patience, my dear boy," gravely spoke the little man of science, busily studying those eddying currents like one seeking a fairly safe method of extrication from peril. "It may come far sooner than you think, and with results more disastrous than feeble words can tell. We surely are a burden such as a tornado must be wholly unaccustomed to, and I really believe these alternations are spasmodic efforts of the cloud itself to vomit us forth; hence you were nearer right than you thought in making use of that expression."

Just then came a rush of icy air, and Bruno pantingly cried:

"I'm swelling up - like Aesop's - bullfrog!"

CHAPTER IV.

THE PROFESSOR'S LITTLE EXPERIMENT.

Again those involuntary riders of the tornado were tossed violently to and fro in their seemingly frail ship, while the balloon itself appeared threatened with instant dissolution, those eddying currents growing broken and far less regular in action, while the fierce tumult grew in sound and volume a thousandfold.

All around the air-ship now showed ugly debris, limbs and boughs and even whole trunks of giant trees being whirled upward and outward, each moment menacing the vessel with total destruction, yet as frequently vanishing without infringing seriously upon their curious prison.

Sand and dirt and fragments of shattered rock whistled by in an apparently unending shower, only with reversed motion, flying upward in place of shooting downward to earth itself.

Speech was utterly impossible under the circumstances, and the fate-tossed voyagers could only cling fast to the hand-rail, and hold those precious air-tubes in readiness for the worst.

Never before had either of the trio heard such a deafening crash and uproar, and little wonder if they thought this surely must herald the crack of doom!

The tornado seemed to reel backward, as though repulsed by

an immovable obstacle, and then, while the din was a bit less deafening, Professor Featherwit contrived to make himself heard, through screaming at the top of his voice:

"The mountain range, I fancy! It's a battle to the -"

That sentence was perforce left incomplete, since the storm-demon gave another mad plunge to renew the battle, bringing on a repetition of that drunken swaying so upsetting to both mind and body.

A few seconds thus, then the tornado conquered, or else rose higher in partial defeat, for their progress was resumed, and comparative quiet reigned again.

The higher clouds curved backward, affording a wider view of the heavens far above, and, as all eyes turned instinctively in that direction, Bruno involuntarily exclaimed:

"Still daylight! I thought - how long has this lasted?"

"It's the middle o' next week; no less!" positively affirmed his brother. "Don't tell me! We've been in here a solid month, by my watch!"

Instead of making reply such as might have been expected from one of his mathematical exactness, Professor Featherwit gave a cry of dismay, while hurriedly moving to and fro in their contracted quarters, for the time being forgetful of all other than this, his great loss.

"What is it, uncle Phaeton?" asked Bruno, rising to his knees in natural anxiety. "Surely nothing worse than has already happened to us?"

"Worse? What could be worse than losing for ever - the camera, boys; where is the camera, I ask you?"

Certainly not where the professor was looking, and even as he roared forth that query, his heart told him the sad truth; past doubting, the instrument upon whose aid he relied to place upon record these marvellous facts, so that all mankind might see and have full faith, was lost, - thrown from the aerostat, to meet with certain destruction, when the vessel first came within the tornado's terrible clutch.

"Gone, - lost, - and now who will believe that we ever - oh, this is enough to crush one's very soul!" mourned the professor, throwing up his hands, and sinking back to the floor of the flying-machine in a limp and disheartened heap for the time being.

Neither Bruno nor Waldo could fully appreciate that grief, since thoughts and care for self were still the ruling passion with both; but once more they were called upon to do battle with the swaying of the winds, and once again were they saved only through that life-giving cylinder of compressed air.

Presently, the heart-broken professor rallied, as was his nature, and, with a visible effort putting his great loss behind him, endeavoured to cheer up his comrades in peril.

"So far we have passed through all danger without receiving material injury, - to ourselves, I mean, - and surely it is not too much to hope for eventual escape?" he said, earnestly, pressing the hands of his nephews, by way of additional encouragement.

"Yes," hesitated Bruno, with an involuntary shiver, as he glanced around them upon those furiously boiling clouds, then cast an eye upward, towards yonder clear sky. "Yes, but - in what manner?"

"What'll we do when the cyclone goes bu'st?" cut in Waldo, with disagreeable bluntness. "It can't go on for ever, and when it splits up, - where will we be then?"

"I wish it lay within my power to give you full assurance on all points, my dear boys," the professor made reply. "I only wish I could ensure your perfect safety by giving my own poor remnant of life -"

"No, no, uncle Phaeton!" cried the brothers, in a single breath.

"How cheerfully, if I only might!" insisted the professor, his homely face wearing an expression of blended regret and unbounded affection. "But for me you would never have encountered these perils, nor ever -"

Again he was interrupted by the brothers, and forced to leave that regret unspoken to the end.

"Only for you, uncle Phaeton, what would have become of us when we were left without parents, home, fortune? Only for you, taking us in and treating us as though of your own flesh and blood -"

"As you are, my good lads! Let it pass, then, but I must say that I do wish - well, well, let it pass, then!"

A brief silence, which was spent in gripping hands and with eyes giving pledges of love and undying confidence; then Professor Featherwit spoke again, in an entirely different vein.

"If nothing else, we have exploded one fallacy which has never met with contradiction, so far as my poor knowledge goes."

"And that is - what, uncle Phaeton?"

"Observe, my lads," with a wave of his hand towards those whirling walls, and then making a downward motion. "You see that we are floating in a partial vacuum, yet where there is air sufficient to preserve life under difficulties. And by looking downward - careful that you don't fall overboard through dizziness, though!"

"Looks as though we were floating just above a bed of ugly

wind!" declared Waldo, after taking a look below.

"Precisely; the aerostat rests upon an air-cushion amply solid enough to sustain far more than our combined weight. But what is the generally accepted view, my dear boys?"

"You tell, for we don't know how," frankly acknowledged Waldo.

"Thanks. Yet you are now far wiser than all of the scientists who have written and published whole libraries concerning these storm formations, but whose fallacies we are now fully prepared to explode, once for all, through knowledge won by personal investigation - ahem!"

Strange though it may appear, the professor forgot the mutual danger by which they were surrounded, and trotted off on his hobby-horse in blissful pride, paying no attention to the hideous uproar going on, only raising his voice higher to make it heard by his youthful auditors.

"The common belief is that, while these tornadoes are hollow, even through the trunk or tongue down to its contact with the earth, that hollow is caused by a constant suction, through which a steady stream of debris is flowing, to be sown broad-cast for miles around after emerging from the open top of the so-called balloon."

"But it isn't at all like that," eagerly cried Waldo, pointing to where the fragments were flowing upward through those walls themselves, yet far enough from that hollow interior to be but indistinctly seen save on rare occasions. "Look at 'em scoot, will ye? Oh, if we could only climb up like that!"

Professor Featherwit was keenly watching and closely studying that very phenomena through all, and now he gave a queer little chuckle, as he nodded his head with vigour, before dryly speaking.

"Well, it might be done; yes, it might be done, and that with no very serious difficulty, my lad."

"How? Why not try it on, then?"

"To meet with instant death outside?" sharply queried Bruno. "It would be suicidal to make the attempt, even if we could; which I doubt."

Waldo gave a sudden cry, pointing upward where, far above that destructive storm, could be seen a brace of buzzards floating on motionless wings, wholly undisturbed by the tumult below.

"If we were only like that!" the lad cried, longingly. "If a flying-machine could be built like those turkey-buzzards! I wish - well, I do suppose they're about the nastiest varmints ever hatched, but just now I'd be willing to swap, and wouldn't ask any boot, either!"

Apparently the professor paid no attention to this boyish plaint, for he was fumbling in the locker, then withdrew his hand and uncoiled an ordinary fish-line, with painted float attached.

Before either brother could ask a question, or even give a guess at his purpose, Professor Phaeton flung hook and cork into those circling currents, only to have the whole jerked violently out of his grip, the line flying upward, to vanish from the sight of all.

That jerk was powerful enough to cut through the skin of his hand, but the professor chuckled like one delighted, as he sucked away the few drops of blood before adding:

"I knew it! It CAN be done, and if the worst should come to pass, why should it not be done?"

Before an answer could be vouchsafed by either of the

brothers, the pall swooped down upon them once more, and again the supply of natural air was shut off, while their vessel was rocked and swayed crazily, just as though the delayed end was at last upon them.

For several minutes this torture endured, each second of which appeared to be an hour to those imperilled beings, who surely must have perished, as they lay pinned fast to the floor of the aerostat by that pitiless weight, only for the precious air-tubes in connection with that cylinder of compressed air.

After a seeming age of torment the awful pressure was relaxed, leaving the trio gasping and shivering, as they lay side by side, barely conscious that life lingered, for the moment unable to lift hand or head to aid either self or another.

In spite of his far greater age, Professor Featherwit was first to rally, and his voice was about the first thing distinguished by the brothers, as their powers began to rally.

"Shall we take our chances, dear boys?" the professor was saying, in earnest tones. "I believe there is a method of escaping from this hell-chamber, although of what may lie beyond -"

"It can't well be worse than this!" huskily gasped Bruno.

"Anything - everything - just to get out o' here!" supplemented Waldo, for once all spirits subdued.

"It may be death for us all, even if we do get outside," gravely warned the professor. "Bear that in mind, dear boys. It may be that not one of us will escape with life, after -"

"How much better to remain here?" interrupted Bruno. "I felt death would be a mercy - then! And I'd risk anything, everything, rather than go through such another ordeal! I say, - escape!"

JOSEPH E. BADGER, JR.

"Me too, all over!" vigorously decided Waldo, lifting himself to both knees as he added: "Tell us what to do, and here I am, on deck, uncle."

Even now Professor Phaeton hesitated, his eyes growing dimmer than usual as they rested upon one face after the other, for right well he knew how deadly would be the peril thus invited.

But, as the brothers repeated their cry, he turned away to swiftly knot a strong trail-rope to a heavy iron grapnel, leaving the other end firmly attached to a stanchion built for that express purpose.

"Hold fast, if you value life at all, dear boys!" he warned, then added: "Heaven be kind to you, even if my life pays the forfeit! Now!"

Without further delay, he cast the heavy grapnel into that mass of boiling vapour, then fell flat, as an awful jerk was given the aerostat.

CHAPTER V.

THE PROFESSOR'S UNKNOWN LAND.

There was neither time nor opportunity for taking notes, for that long rope straightened out in the fraction of a second, throwing all prostrate as the flying-machine was jerked upward with awful force.

All around them raged and roared the mighty winds, while missiles of almost every description pelted and pounded both machine and inmates during those few seconds of extraordinary peril.

Fortunately neither the professor nor his nephews could fairly realise just what was taking place, else their brains would hardly have stood the test; and fortunately, too, that ordeal was not protracted.

A hideous experience while it lasted, those vicious currents dragging the aerostat upward out of the air-chamber by means of grapnel and rope, then casting all far away in company with wrecked trees and bushes, and even solider materials, all shrouded for a time in dust and debris, which hindered the eyesight of both uncle and nephews.

Through it all the brothers were dimly aware of one fact uncle Phaeton was shrilly bidding them cling fast and have courage.

All at once they felt as though vomited forth from a volcano which alternately breathed fire and ice, the clear light of evening bursting upon their aching, smarting eyes with actual pain, while that horrid roar of warring elements seemed to pass away in the distance, leaving them - where, and how?

"We're falling to - merciful heavens! Hold fast, all!" screamed the professor, desperately striving to regain full command of their air-ship. "The tiller is jammed, but -"

To all seeming, the aerostat had sustained some fatal damage during that brief eruption caused by the professor's little experiment, for it was pitching drunkenly end for end, refusing to obey the hand of its builder, bearing all to certain death upon the earth far below.

Half stupefied with fear, the brothers clung fast to the life-line and glared downward, noting, in spite of themselves, how swiftly yonder dark tree-tops and gray crags were shooting heavenward to meet them and claim the sacrifice.

With fierce energy Professor Featherwit jerked and wrenched at the steering-gear, uttering words such as had long been foreign to his lips, but then - just when destruction appeared inevitable - a wild cry burst from his lungs, as a broken bit of native wood came away in his left hand, leaving the lever free as of old!

And then, with a dizzying swoop and rapid recovery, the gallant air-ship came back to an even keel, sailing along with old-time grace and ease, barely in time to avoid worse mishap as the crest of a tall tree was brushed in their passage.

"Saved, - saved, my lads!" screamed the professor, as his heart-pet soared upward once more until well past the danger-line. "Safe and sound through all, - praises be unto the Lord, our Father!"

Neither brother spoke just then, for they lay there in half stupor, barely able to realise the wondrous truth: that their lives had surely been spared them, even as by a miracle!

That swooping turn now brought their faces towards the tornado, which was at least a couple of miles distant, rapidly making that distance greater even while continuing its work of destruction.

"And we - were in it!" huskily muttered Bruno, his lids closing with a shiver, as he averted his face, unwilling to see more.

"Heap sight worse than being in the soup, too, if anybody asks you," declared Waldo, beginning to rally both in strength and in spirit. "But - what's the matter with the old ship, uncle Phaeton?"

For the aerostat was indulging itself in sundry distressing gyrations, pretty much as a boy's kite swoops from side to side, when lacking in tail-ballast, while the professor seemed unable to keep the machine under complete control.

"Nothing serious, only - hold fast, all! I believe 'twould be as well to make our descent, for fear something - steady!"

Just ahead there appeared a more than usually open space in the forest, and, quite as much by good luck as through actual skill, Professor Featherwit succeeded in making a landing with no more serious mishap than sundry bruises and a little extra teeth-jarring.

As quickly as possible, both Bruno and Waldo pitched themselves out of the partially disabled aeromotor, the elder brother grasping the grapnel and taking a couple of turns of the strong rope around a convenient tree-trunk, lest the ship escape them altogether.

"No need, my gallant boy!" assured the professor, an instant later. "All is well, - all IS well, thanks to an over-ruling Providence!"

In spite of this expressed confidence, he hurriedly looked over his pet machine, taking note of such injuries as had been received during that remarkable journey, only giving over when fairly satisfied that all damage might be readily made good, after which the aerostat would be as trustworthy as upon its first voyage on high.

Then, grasping the brothers each by a hand, he smiled genially, then lifted eyes heavenward, to a moment later sink upon his knees with bowed head and hands folded across his bosom.

Bruno and Waldo imitated his action, and, though no audible words were spoken, never were more heartfelt prayers sent upward, never more grateful thanks given unto the Most High.

Boy, youth, and man alike seemed fairly awed into silence for the next few minutes, unable to so soon cast off the spell which had fallen upon them, one and each, when realising how mercifully their lives had been spared, even after all earthly hope had been abandoned.

As usual, however, Waldo was first to rally, and, after silently moving around the aerostat, upon which the professor was already busily at work by the last gleams of the vanished sun, he paused, legs separated, and hands thrust deep into pockets, head perking on one side as he spoke, drawlingly:

"I say, uncle Phaeton?"

"What is it, Waldo?"

"It'll never do to breathe even a hint of all this, will it?"

"Why so, pray?"

"Whoever heard it would swear we were bald-headed liars right from Storytown! And yet, - did it really happen, or have I been dreaming all the way through?"

Professor Featherwit gave a brief, dry chuckle at this, rising erect to cast a deliberate glance around their present location, then speaking:

"Without I am greatly mistaken, my dear boy, you will have still other marvellous happenings to relate ere we return to what is, rightfully or wrongfully, called civilisation."

"Is that so? Then you really reckon -"

"For one thing, my lad, we are now fairly entered upon a terra incognita, so far as our own race is concerned. In other words, - behold, the Olympics!"

Both Bruno and Waldo cast their eyes around, but only a circumscribed view was theirs. The shades of evening were settling fast, and on all sides they could see but mighty trees, rugged rocks, a mountain stream from whose pebbly bed came a soothing murmur.

"Nothing so mighty much to brag of, anyway," irreverently quoth Waldo, after that short-lived scrutiny. "It wouldn't fetch a dollar an acre at auction, and for my part, - wonder when the gong will sound for supper?"

That blunt hint was effective, and, letting the subject drop for the time being, even the professor joined in the hurry for an evening meal, to which one and all felt able to do full justice.

Although some rain had fallen at this point as well, no serious difficulty was experienced in kindling a fire, while Waldo had little trouble in heaping up a bounteous supply of fuel.

Through countless ages the forest monarchs had been shedding their superfluous boughs, while here and there lay an entire tree, overthrown by some unknown power, and upon which the brothers made heavy requisition.

Professor Featherwit took from the locker a supply of tinned goods, together with a patent coffee-pot and frying-pan, so convenient where space is scarce and stowage-room precious.

With water from the little river, it took but a few minutes more to scent the evening with grateful fumes, after which the adventurous trio squatted there in the ruddy glow, eating, sipping, chatting, now and again forced to give thanks for their really miraculous preservation after all human hopes had been exhausted.

Although Professor Featherwit was but little less thankful for the wondrous leniency shown them, he could not altogether refrain from mourning the loss of his camera, with its many snap-shots at the tornado itself, to say nothing of what he might have secured in addition, while riding the storm so marvellously.

More to take his thoughts away from that loss than through actual curiosity in the subject offered by way of substitute, Bruno asked for further light upon the so-called terra incognita.

"Of course it isn't really an unknown land, though, uncle Phaeton?" he added, almost apologetically. "In this age, and upon our own continent, such a thing is among the impossibilities."

"Indeed? And, pray, how long since has it been that you would, with at least equal positivity, have declared it impossible to enter a tornado while in wildest career, yet emerge from it with life and limb intact?"

"Yes, uncle, but - this is different, by far."

"In one sense, yes; in another, no," affirmed the professor, with emphatic nod, brushing the tips of his fingers together, as he moved back to assume a more comfortable position inside the air-ship, then quickly preparing a pipe and tobacco for his regular after-meal smoke.

A brief silence, then the professor spoke, clearly, distinctly:

"Washington has her great unknown land, quite as much as has the interior of Darkest Africa, my boys, besides enjoying this peculiar advantage: while adventurous white men have traversed those benighted regions in every direction, even though little permanent good may have been accomplished, this terra incognita remains virgin in that particular sense of the word."

"You mean, uncle?"

"That here in the Olympic region you see what is literally an unknown, unexplored scope of country, as foreign to the foot of mankind as it was countless ages gone by. So far as history reads, neither white man nor red has ever ventured fairly within these limits; a mountainous waste which rises from the level country, within ten or fifteen miles of the Straits of San Juan de Fuca, in the north, the Pacific Ocean in the west, Hood's Canal in the east, and the barren sand-hills lying to the far south.

"This irregular range is known upon the map as the Olympics, and, rising to the height of from six to eight thousand feet, shut in a vast unexplored area.

"The Indians have never penetrated it, so far as can be ascertained, for their traditions say that it is inhabited by a very fierce tribe of warriors, before whose might and strange weapons not one of the coast tribes can stand."

"One of the Lost Tribes of Israel, shouldn't wonder," drawlingly volunteered Waldo, stifling a yawn, and forced to rub his inflamed eyes with a surreptitious paw.

Professor Featherwit, though plainly absorbed in his curious theory, was yet quick to detect this evidence of weariness, and laughed a bit, with change of both tone and manner, as he spoke further:

"That forms but a partial introductory to my lecture, dear lads, but perhaps it might be as well to postpone the rest for a more propitious occasion. You have undergone sore trials, both of - Hark!"

Some sound came to his keen ears, which the brothers failed to catch, but as they bent their heads in listening, another noise came, which proved startling enough, in all conscience, - a shrill, maniacal screech, which sent cold chills running races up each spine.

CHAPTER VI.

A BRACE OF UNWELCOME VISITORS.

Instinctively the brothers drew nearer each other, as though for mutual protection, each one letting hand drop to belt where a revolver was habitually carried, but which was lacking now, thanks to the great haste with which they had taken wing at the approach of the tornado.

"What is it? What can it mean?" asked Bruno and Waldo, almost in the same breath, as those fierce echoes died away in the distance.

Professor Featherwit made no immediate reply, but by the glow of yonder camp-fire he fumbled inside the magic locker, fetching forth firearms, then speaking in hushed tones:

"Wait. Listen for - I knew it!"

From the opposite quarter came what might easily have been an echo of that first wild screech, only louder, longer, more savage, if such a thing be possible.

Prepared though they now were, neither brother could refrain from shrinking and shuddering, so hideously that cry sounded in their ears. But their uncle spoke in cool, clear tones:

"There is nothing supernatural about that, my lads. A panther or mountain lion, I dare say, scenting the fumes of our

JOSEPH E. BADGER, JR.

cookery, and coming to claim a share."

"Then it isn't - Nothing spookish, uncle Phaeton?" ventured Waldo, in slightly unsteady tones.

The professor gave swift assurance upon that point, and, rallying as few youngsters would have done under like circumstances, the brothers grasped the weapons supplied their hands, waiting and watching for what was to come.

Once, twice, thrice those savage calls echoed far and wide, but with each repetition losing a portion of their terrors; and knowing now that prowling beasts surely were drawing nigh the camp-fire, the flying machine was abandoned by the trio, all drawing closer to the fire, which might prove no slight protection against attack.

Then followed a period of utter silence, during which their eyes roved restlessly around, striving to sight the four-footed enemy ere an actual attack could be made.

Professor Featherwit was first to glimpse a pair of greenish eyes in silent motion, and, giving a low hiss of warning to his nephews, that same sound serving to check further progress on the part of the wild beast, his short rifle came to a level, then emitted a peculiar sound.

Only the keenest of ears could have noted that, for only the fraction of an instant later followed a sharp explosion, the darkness beyond being briefly lit up by a yellowish glare.

"That's enough, - beware its mate!" cried the professor, keenly alert for whatever might ensue; but the words were barely across his lips when, with a vicious snarl, a furry shape came flying through the air, knocking Featherwit over as he instinctively ducked his head with arm flying up as additional guard.

Both man and beast came very near falling into the fire itself, and there ensued a wild, confused scramble, out of which the brothers singled their enemy, Waldo opening fire with a revolver, at close range, each shot causing the lion to yell and snarl most ferociously.

A cat-like recovery, then the fatal leap might have followed, for the confused professor was rising to his feet again, fairly in front of the enraged brute; but ere worse came, Waldo and Bruno were to the rescue, one firing as rapidly as possible, his brother driving a keen-bladed knife to the very hilt just back of that quivering forearm.

One mad wrestle, in which both lads were overthrown, then the gaunt and muscular brute stretched its length in a shivering throe, dead even while it strove to slay.

Just as the professor hurried to the front, beseeching his boys to keep out of peril if they loved him; at which Waldo laughed outright, although never had he felt a warmer love for the same odd-speaking, queer-acting personage than right at that moment.

"I'm all right; how's it with you, sir? And - Bruno?"

"Without a scratch to remember it by," promptly asserted the elder brother, likewise regaining his feet and taking hasty account of stock. "No fault of his, though!" giving that carcass a kick as he spoke. "My gracious! I caught just one glimpse of them, and I was ready to make affidavit that each fang would measure a foot, while his claws -"

"Would pass through an elephant and clinch on the other side," declared Waldo, stooping far enough to lift one of those armed paws. "But, I say, Bruno, how awfully they have shrunk, since then!"

Whether so intended or not, this characteristic break caused a mutual laugh, and, as there was neither sound nor sign of further danger from like source, one and all satisfied their curiosity by minutely inspecting the huge brute, stirring up the fire for that purpose.

"An ugly customer, indeed, if we had given him anything like a fair show," gravely uttered the professor. "Only for your prompt assistance, my dear boys, what would have become of poor me?"

"We acted on our own account, as well, please remember, uncle. And even so, after all you have done for us since -"

"What was it you shot at, uncle Phaeton?" interrupted Waldo, who was constitutionally averse to aught which savoured of sentiment. "Another one of these - little squirrels, was it?"

Snatching up a blazing brand, the lad moved off in that direction, whirling the torch around his head until it burst into clear flame, then lowering it closer to a bloody heap of fur and powerful limbs, to give a short ejaculation of wondering awe.

It was a headless body upon which he gazed, ragged fragments of skin and a few splinters of bone alone remaining to tell that a solid skull had so recently been thereon.

Professor Phaeton gave another of his peculiar little chuckles, as he drew near, then patted the compact little rifle with which he had wrought such extraordinary work: a weapon of his own invention, as were the dynamite-filled shells to match.

"Although I am rather puny myself, boys, with this neat little contrivance I could fairly well hold my own against man or beast," he modestly averred.

"A modern David," gravely added Bruno, while Waldo chimed in with:

"What a dandy Jack the Giant-killer you would have been, uncle Phaeton, if you had only lived in the good old days! I wish - and yet I don't, either! Of course, it might have been jolly old sport right then, but now, - where'd I be, to-day?"

"A day on which has happened a miracle far more marvellous than all that has been set down in fairyland romance, my dear son," earnestly spoke the professor. "And when the astounding truth shall have been published, broadcast, throughout all Christendom, what praises -"

"How thoroughly we shall be branded liars, and falsificationers from 'way up the crick'!" exploded the youngster, making a wry grimace and moving on to view the headless lion from a different standpoint.

"He means well, uncle Phaeton," assured Bruno, in lowered tones. "He would not knowingly hurt your feelings, sir, but - may I speak out?"

"Why not?" quickly. "Surely I am not one to stand in awe of, lad?"

"One to be loved and reverenced, rather," with poorly hidden emotion; then rallying, to add, "But when one finds it impossible to realise all that has happened this afternoon, when one feels afraid to even make an effort at such belief, how can the boy be blamed for feeling that all others would pronounce us mad or - wilful liars?"

Professor Phaeton saw the point, and made a wry grimace while roughing up his pompadour and brushing his closely trimmed beard with doubtful hand. After all, was the whole truth to be ever spoken?

"Well, well, we can determine more clearly after fully weighing the subject," he said, turning back towards the flying-machine. "And, after all, what has happened to us thus far may not seem so utterly incredible after our explorations are completed."

"Of this region, do you mean, sir?"

"Of the Olympic mountains, and all their mountainous chain may encompass, - yes," curtly spoke the man of hopes, stepping inside the aerostat to perfect his arrangements for the night.

Waldo took greater pleasure in viewing the mountain lion towards whose destruction he had so liberally contributed, but when he spoke of removing the skin, Bruno objected.

"Why take so much trouble for nothing, Waldo? Even if we could stow the pelts away on board, they would make a far from agreeable burden. And if what I fancy lies before us is to come true, the more lightly we are weighted, the more likely we are to come safely to - well, call it civilisation, just for a change."

"Then you believe that uncle Phaeton is really in earnest about exploring this region, Bruno?"

"He most assuredly is. Did you ever know him to speak idly, or to be otherwise than in earnest, Waldo?"

"Well, of course uncle is all right, but - sometimes -"

A friendly palm slipped over those lips, cutting short the speech which might perchance have left a sting behind. And yet the worthy professor had no more enthusiastic acolyte than this same reckless speaking youngster, when the truth was all told.

Leaving the animals where they had fallen, for the time being, the brothers passed over to where rested the aeromotor, finding the professor busily engaged in rigging up a series of fine wires, completely surrounding the flying-machine, save one narrow, gate-like arrangement.

"Beginning to feel as though you could turn in for all night, eh, my boys?" came his cheery greeting.

"Well, somehow I do feel as though 'the sandman' had been making his rounds rather earlier than customary," dryly said

Waldo, winking rapidly. "I believe there must have been a bit more wind astir to-day than common, although neither of you may have noticed the fact."

Professor Featherwit chuckled softly while at work, but neither he nor Bruno made reply in words. And then, his arrangements perfected save for closing the circuit, which could only be done after all hands had entered the air-ship, he spoke to the point:

"Come, boys. You've had a rough bit of experience this day, and there may be still further trouble in store, here in this unknown land. Better make sure of a full night's rest, and thus have a reserve fund to draw upon in case of need."

There was plenty of sound common sense in this adjuration, and, only taking time to procure a can of fresh water from yonder stream, the two youngsters stepped within that charmed circle, permitting their uncle to close the circuit, and then test the queer contrivance to make sure all was working nicely.

A confused sound broke forth, resembling the faraway tooting of tin horns, which blended inharmoniously with the ringing of nearer bells, all producing a noise which was warranted to arouse the heaviest sleeper from his soundest slumber.

"That will give fair warning in case any intruder drifts this way," declared the professor, chucklingly, then sinking down and wrapping himself up in a close-woven blanket, similar to those employed by the boys.

"Even a ghost, or a goblin, do you reckon, uncle Phaeton?"

"Should such attempt to intrude, yes. Go to sleep, you young rascal!"

But that proved to be far more readily spoken than lived up to. Not but that the brothers were weary, jaded, and sore of muscle enough to make even the thought of slumber agreeable; but their recent experience had been so thrilling, so nerve-straining, so far apart from the ordinary routine of life, that hours passed ere either lad could fairly lose himself in sleep.

Still, when unconsciousness did steal over their weary brains, it proved to be all the more complete, and after that neither Bruno nor Waldo stirred hand or foot until, well after the dawn of a new day, Professor Featherwit shook first one and then the other, crying shrilly:

"Turn out, youngsters! A new day, and plenty of work to be done!"

CHAPTER VII.

THE PROFESSOR'S GREAT ANTICIPATIONS.

A stretch and a yawn, which in Waldo's case ended in a prolonged howl, which would not have disgraced either of their four-footed visitors of the past evening, then the brothers Gillespie sprung forth from the flying-machine, entering upon a race for the brawling mountain stream, "shedding" their garments as they ran.

"First man in!" cried Bruno, whose clothes seemed to slip off the more readily; but Waldo was not to be outdone so easily, and, reckless of the consequences, he plunged into the eddying pool, with fully half of his daylight rig still in place.

The water proved to be considerably deeper than either brother had anticipated, and Waldo vanished from sight for a few seconds, then reappearing with lusty puff and splutter, shaking the pearly drops from his close-clipped curls, while ranting:

"Another vile fabrication nailed to the standard of truth, and clinched by the hammer of - ouch!"

A wild flounder, then the youngster fairly doubled himself up, acting so strangely that Bruno gave a little cry of alarm; but ere the elder brother could take further action, Waldo swung his right arm upward and outward, sending a goodly sized trout flashing through the air to the shore, crying in boyish enthusiasm:

"Glory in great chunks! I want to camp right here for a year to come! Will ye look at that now?"

Bruno had to dodge that writhing missile, and, before he could fairly recover himself, Waldo had floundered ashore, leaving a yeasty turmoil in his wake, but then throwing up a dripping and, and speaking in an exaggerated whisper:

"Whist, boy! On your life, not so much as the ghost of a whimper! The hole's ramjammed chuck full of trout, and we'll have a meal fit for the gods if - where's my fishing tackle?"

Bruno picked up the trout, so queerly brought to light, really surprised, but feigning still further, as he made his examination.

"It really IS a trout, and - how long have you carried this about in your clothes, Waldo Gillespie?"

"Not long enough for you to build a decent joke over it, brother mine. Just happened so. Tried to ram its nose in one of my pockets, and of course I had to take him in out of the wet. Pool's just full of them, too, and I wouldn't wonder if - oh, quit your talking, and do something, can't you, boy?"

Vigorously though he spoke, Waldo wound up with a shiver and sharp chatter of teeth as the fresh morning air struck through his dripping garments. He gave a coltish prance, as he turned to seek his fishing tackle; but, unfortunately for his hopes of speedy sport, the professor was nigh enough to both see and hear, and at once took charge of the reckless youngster.

"Wet to the hide, and upon an empty stomach, too! You foolish child! Come, strip to the buff, and put on some of these garments until - here by the fire, Waldo."

And thus taken in tow, the lad was forced to slowly but

thoroughly toast his person beside the freshly started fire, ruefully watching his brother deftly handle rod and line, in a remarkably short space of time killing trout enough to furnish all with a bounteous meal.

"And I was the discoverer, while you reap all the credit, have all the fun!" dolefully lamented Waldo, when the catch was displayed with an ostentation which may have covered just a tiny bit of malice. "I'll put a tin ear on you, Amerigo Vespucius!"

"All right; we'll have a merry go together, after you've cleaned the trout for cooking, lad," laughed his elder.

Waldo gazed reproachfully into that bright face for a brief space, then bowed head in joined hands, to sob in heartfelt fashion, his sturdy frame shaking with poorly suppressed grief - or mirth?

Bruno passed an arm caressingly over those shoulders, murmuring words of comfort, earnestly promising to never sin again in like manner, provided he could find forgiveness now. And then, with deft touch, that same hand held his garment far enough for its mate to let slip a wriggling trout adown his brother's back.

Waldo howled and jumped wildly, as the cold morsel slipped along his spine, and ducking out of reach, the elder jester called back:

"Land him, boy, and you've caught another fish!"

Although laughing heartily himself, Professor Featherwit deemed it a part of wisdom to interfere now, and, ere long, matters quieted down, all hands engaged in preparing the morning meal, for which all teeth were now fairly on edge.

If good nature had been at all disturbed, long before that breakfast was despatched it was fully restored, and of the trio,

Waldo appeared to be the most enthusiastic over present prospects.

"Why, just think of it, will you?" he declaimed, as well as might be with mouth full of crisply fried mountain trout. "where the game comes begging for you to bowl it over, and the very fish try to jump into your pockets -"

"Or down your back, Amerigo," interjected Bruno, with a grin.

"Button up, or you'll turn to be a Sorry-cus - tomer, old man," came the swift retort, with a portentous frown. "But, joking aside, why not? With such hunting and fishing, I'd be willing to sign a contract for a round year in this region."

"To say nothing of exploration, and such discoveries as naturally attend upon -"

"Then you really mean it all, uncle Phaeton?"

Leaning back far enough to pluck a handful of green leaves, which fairly well served the purpose of a napkin, Professor Featherwit brought forth pipe and pouch, maintaining silence until the fragrant tobacco was well alight. Then he gave a vigorous nod of his head, to utter:

"It has been the dearest dream of my life for more years gone by than you would readily credit, my lads; or, in fact, than I would be wholly willing to confess. And it was with an eye single to this very adventure that I laboured to devise and perfect yonder machine."

"A marvel in itself, uncle Phaeton. Only for that, where would we have been, yesterday?" seriously spoke the elder Gillespie.

"I know where we wouldn't have been: inside that blessed cy-nado!"

"Nor here, where you can catch brook trout in your clothes without the trouble of taking them off, youngster."

"And where you'll catch a precious hiding, without you let up harping on that old string; it's way out of tune already, old man,"

"Tit for tat. Excuse us, please, uncle Phaeton. We're like colts in fresh pasture, this morning," brightly apologised Bruno, for both.

Apparently the professor paid no attention to that bit of sparring between his nephews, staring into the glowing camp-fire with eyes which surely saw more than yellow coals or ruddy flames could picture; eyes which burned and sparkled with all the fires of distant youth.

"The dearest dream of all my life!" he repeated, in half dreamy tones, only to rouse himself, with a a start and shoulder shake, an instant later, forcing a bright smile as he glanced from face to face. "And why not? How better could my last years be employed than in piercing the clouds of mystery, and doubt, and superstition, with which this vast tract has been enveloped for uncounted ages?"

"Is it really so unknown, then, uncle Phaeton?" hesitatingly asked Bruno, touched, in spite of himself, by that intensely earnest tone and expression. "Of course, I know what the Indians say; they are full of a rude sort of superstitious awe, which -"

"Which is one of the surest proofs that truth forms a foundation for that very superstition," quickly interjected the professor. "It is an undisputed fact that there are hundreds upon hundreds of square miles of terra incognita, lying in this corner of Washington Territory. No white man ever fairly penetrated these wilds, even so far as we may have been carried while riding the tornado. Or, if so, he assuredly has never returned, or made known his discoveries."

JOSEPH E. BADGER, JR.

"Provided there was anything beyond the ordinary to see or experience, shouldn't we add, uncle?" suggested Waldo, modestly.

"There is, - there must be! No matter how wildly improbable their traditions may seem in our judgment, it only takes calm investigation to bring a fair foundation to light. In regard to this vast scope of country, go where you will among the natives, question whom you see fit, as to its secrets, and you will meet with the same results: a deep-seated awe, a belief which cannot be shaken, that here strange monsters breed and flourish, matched in magnitude and power by an armed race of human beings, before whose awful might other tribes are but as ants in the pathway of an elephant."

Waldo let escape a low, prolonged whistle of mingled wonder and incredulity, but Bruno gave him a covert kick, himself too deeply interested to bear with a careless interruption just then.

"Of course there may be something of exaggeration in all this," admitted the enthusiastic professor. "Undoubtedly, there is at least a fair spice of that; but, even so, enough remains to both waken and hold our keenest interest. Listen, and take heed, my good lads.

"You have often enough, of late days, noticed these mountains, and if you remark their altitude, the vast scope of country they dominate, the position they fill, you must likewise realise one other fact: that an immense quantity of snow in winter, rain in spring and autumn, surely must fall throughout the Olympics. Understand?"

"Certainly; why not, uncle Phaeton?"

"Then tell me this: where does all the moisture go to? What becomes of the surplus waters? For it is an acknowledged fact that, though rivers and brooks surely exist in the Olympics, not one of either flows away from this wide tract of country!"

The professor paused for a minute, to let his words take full effect, then even more positively proceeded:

"You may say, what I have had others offer by way of solution, that all is drained into a mighty inland sea or enormous lake. Granting so much, which I really believe to be the truth as far as it goes, why does that lake never overflow? Of all that surely must drain into its basin, be that enormously wide and deep as it may, how much could ordinary evaporation dispose of? Only an infinitesimal portion; scarcely worth mentioning in such connection. Then, - what becomes of the surplusage?"

Another pause, during which neither Gillespie ventured a solution; then the professor offered his own suggestion:

"It must flow off in some manner, and what other manner can that be than - through a subterranean connection with the Pacific Ocean?"

Bruno gave a short ejaculation at this, while Waldo broke forth in words, after his own particular fashion:

"Jules Verne redivivus! Why can't WE take a trip through the centre of the earth, or - or - any other little old thing like that?"

"With the tank of compressed air as a life-preserver?" laughed Bruno, in turn. "That might serve, but; unfortunately, we have only the one, and we are three in number, boy."

"Only two, now; I'm squelched!" sighed the jester, faintly.

If the professor heard, he heeded not. Still staring with vacant gaze into the fire, his face bearing a rapt expression curious to see, he broke into almost unconscious speech:

"An enormous inland sea! Where float the mighty ichthyo-saurus, the megalosaurus, in company with the gigantic plesiosaurus! Upon whose sloping shores disport the enormous mastodon, the stately megatherium, the tremendous - eh?"

For Waldo was now afoot, brandishing a great branch broken from a dead tree, uttering valiant war-whoops, and dealing tremendous blows upon an imaginary enemy, spouting at the top of his voice a frenzied jargon, which neither his auditors nor himself could possibly make sense out of.

Bruno, ever sensitive through his affectionate reverence for their uncle, caught the youngster, and cast him to earth, whereupon Waldo pantingly cried:

"Go on, please, uncle Phaeton. It's next thing to a museum and menagerie combined, just to hear -"

"Will you hush, boy?" demanded Bruno, yet unable to wholly smother a laugh, so ridiculous did it all sound and seem.

But Professor Featherwit declined, his foxy face wrinkling in a bashful laugh. Whether so intended or not, he had been brought down to earth from that dizzy flight, and now was fairly himself again.

"Well, my dear boys, I dare say it seems all a matter of jest and sport to you; yet, after our riding in the centre of a tornado for uncounted miles, coming forth with hardly a scratch or a bruise to show for it all, who dare say such things may not be, even yet?"

"But, - those strange creatures are gone; the last one perished thousands upon thousands of years ago, uncle Phaeton."

"So it is said, and so follows the almost universal belief. Yet I have seen, felt, cooked, tasted, and ate to its last morsel a steak from a mammoth. True, the creature was dead; had been preserved for ages, no doubt, within the glacier which finally cast it forth to human view; yet who would have credited such a discovery, only fifty years ago? He who dared to even hint at such a thing would have been derided and laughed at, pronounced either fool or lunatic. And so, - if we should happen to discover one or all of those supposedly extinct creatures here in this terra incognita, I would be overjoyed rather than astounded."

Bruno looked grave at this conclusion, but Waldo was not so readily impressed, and, with shrugging shoulders, he made answer:

"Well, uncle, I'm not quite so ambitious as all that comes to. May I give you my idea of it all?"

CHAPTER VIII.

A DUEL TO THE DEATH.

Professor Featherwit nodded assent, and, after a brief chuckle, Waldo resumed:

"You can take all those big fellows with the jaw-breaking names, but as for me, smaller game will do. Maybe a fellow couldn't fill his bag quite so full, nor quite so suddenly, but there would be a great deal more sport, and a mighty sight less danger, I take it!"

It was by no means difficult to divine that the professor had not yet spoken all that busied his brain, but the thread was broken, his pipe was out, and, emptying the ashes by tapping pipe-bowl against the heel of his shoe, he rose erect, once more the man of action.

"You will have to clear up, lads, for I must make such few repairs as are necessary to restore the aerostat to a state of efficiency. So long as that remains in serviceable condition, we will always have a method of advance or retreat. Without it - well, I'd rather not think of the alternative."

That dry tone and quiet sentence did more than all else to impress the brothers with a sense of their unique position. Back came the remembrance of all they had gathered concerning this strange scope of country since first settling down fairly within the shadows of the Olympics, there to put that strange machine together, preparing for what was to prove a wonder-tour through many marvellous happenings.

Times beyond counting they had been assured by the natives that no mortal could fairly penetrate that vast wilderness. Natural obstacles were too great for any man to surmount, without saying aught of what lay beyond; of the enormous animals, such as the civilised world never knew or fought with; of the terrible natives, taller than the pines, larger than the hills, more powerful by far than the gods themselves, eager to slay and to devour, - so eager that, at times, living flesh and blood was more grateful than all to their depraved tastes!

"Do you really reckon there is anything in it all, Bruno?" asked the younger brother in lowered tones, glancing across to where their uncle was busily engaged in those comparatively trifling repairs.

"It hardly seems possible, and yet - would the members of four different tribes tell a story so nearly alike, without they had at least a foundation of truth to go upon?"

"That's right. And yet - the inland sea sounds natural enough. We know, too, that there are such things as underground rivers, outside of Jules Verne's yarns. But those animals, - or reptiles, - which?"

"Both, I believe," answered Bruno, with a subdued laugh.

"That's all right, old man. I never was worth a continental when it came to such things. I prefer to live in the present, and so - well, now, will you just look at that old cow!"

In surprise Waldo pointed across to where a bovine shape showed not far beyond the pool at the base of the miniature waterfall; but his brother had a fairer view, and, instantly divining the truth, grasped an arm and hastily whispered:

"Hush, boy; can't you see? It's a buffalo, a hill buffalo, and -"

"Quick! the guns are in the machine! Down, Bruno, and maybe we can get a shot and -"

His eager whisper was cut short, though not by grip of arm or act by his brother. A rumbling roar broke forth from the further side of that mountain stream, and as the dense bushes beyond were violently agitated, the hill buffalo wheeled that way with marvellous rapidity.

Just as a long head and mighty shoulders spread the shrubbery wide apart, jaws opening and lips curling back to lay great teeth bare, while another angry sound, half growl, half snort, only too clearly proclaimed that monster of the mountains, a grizzly bear.

"Smoke o' sacrifice!" gasped Waldo, as the grizzly suddenly upreared its mighty bulk, head wagging, paws waving in queer fashion, lolling tongue lending the semblance of drollery rather than viciousness.

"This way; to your guns, boys!" cautiously called out the professor, whose notice had likewise been caught by those unusual sounds, and who had already armed himself with his pet dynamite gun.

"Careful! He'll make a break for us at first sight, unless - down close, and crawl for it, brother!"

Bruno set the good example, and Waldo was not too proud of spirit to humble himself in like manner. Although this was their first glimpse of "Old Eph" in his native wilds, both brothers entertained a very respectful opinion of his prowess.

Under different circumstances their expectations might have been more fully met, but just now the grizzly seemed wholly occupied with the buffalo bull, whose sturdy bulk and armed front so resolutely opposed his further progress towards that common goal, the pool of water.

The boys quickly reached the flying-machine and gripped the Winchester rifles which Professor Featherwit had drawn forth from the locker at first sight of the dangerous game. Thus armed, they felt ready for whatever might come, and stood watching yonder rivals with growing interest.

"Will you look at that, now?" excitedly breathed Waldo, eyes aglow, as he saw the bull cock its tail on high and tear up the soft soil with one fierce sweep of its cloven hoof, shaking head and giving vent to a low but determined bellow.

"It means a fight unto the death, I think," whispered the professor.

"It's dollars to doughnuts on the bear," predicted Waldo. "Scat, you bull-headed idiot! Don't you know that you're not deuce high to his ace? Can't you see that he can chew you up like -"

"Are you mighty sure of all that, boy?" laughingly cut in Bruno; for at that moment the buffalo made a sudden charge at his upright adversary, knocking the grizzly backward in spite of its viciously flying paws.

"Great Peter on a bender! If I ever - no, I never!"

Even the professor was growing excited, holding the dynamite gun under one arm while gently tapping palms together as an encore.

Naturally enough, their sympathies were with the buffalo, since the odds seemed so immensely against him; but their delight was short-lived, for, instead of following up the advantage so bravely won, the bull fell back to paw and bellow and shake his shaggy front.

With marvellous activity for a brute of his enormous bulk and weight, the grizzly recovered its feet, then lumbered forward with clashing teeth and resounding growls.

JOSEPH E. BADGER, JR.

Nothing loath, the buffalo met that charge, and for a short space of time the struggle was veiled by showers of leaf-mould and damp dirt cast upon the air as the rivals fought for supremacy - and for life.

For that this was destined to be a duel to the very death not one of those spectators could really doubt. That encounter may have been purely accidental, but the creatures fought like enemies of long standing.

As their relative positions changed, the buffalo contrived to get in another vigorous butt, sending bruin end for end down that gentle slope to souse into the pool of water, that cool element cutting short a savage roar of mad fury.

Then the trio of spectators could take notes, and with something of sorrow they saw that the buffalo had already suffered severely, bleeding from numerous great gashes torn by the grizzly's long talons, while one bloody eye dangled below its socket, held only by a thread of sinew.

Nor had bruin escaped without hurt, as all could see when he floundered out of the water, bent upon renewing the duel; but there was little room left for doubting what the ultimate result would be were the animals left to their own devices.

Like all bold, free-hearted lads, Waldo ever sympathised with the weaker, and now, unable to hold his feelings in check, he gave a short cry, levelling his Winchester and opening fire upon the grizzly, just as it won fairly clear of the water.

Stung to fury by those pellets, the brute reared up with a horrid roar, turning as though to charge this new enemy; but ere he could do more, the professor's gun spoke, and as the dynamite shell exploded, bruin fell back a writhing mass, his head literally smashed to pieces.

Heedless of all else, the wounded buffalo charged with lusty bellow, goring that quivering mass with unabated fury, though its life was clearly leaking out through those ghastly cuts and slashes.

A brief pause, then Professor Featherwit swiftly reloaded his gun, sending another shell across the stream, this time more as a boon than as punishment.

Smitten fairly in the forehead, the bull dropped as though beneath a bolt of lightning, life going out without so much as a single struggle or a single pang.

"Twas better thus," declared the professor, as Waldo gave a little ejaculation of dismay. "He must have bled to death in a short time, and this was true mercy. Besides, buffalo meat is very good eating, and the day may come when we shall need all we can get. Who knows?"

After the animals were inspected, and due comment made upon the awfully sure work wrought by the dynamite gun, the professor suggested that, while he was completing repairs upon the aeromotor, the brothers should secure a supply of fish and of flesh, cooking sufficient to provide for several meals, for there was no telling just when they would have an equal chance.

"Just as soon as we can put all in readiness," he continued, "I am going to leave this spot. My first wish is to thoroughly test the aerostat, to make certain it has received no serious injury. Then, if all promises well, I mean to begin our tour of exploration, hoping that we may, at least, find something well worthy the strange reputation given these Olympics by the natives."

Without raising any objections, the brothers fell to work, Bruno looking after the flesh, while Waldo undertook to supply the fish. That was but fair, since he had been cheated out of catching the first mess.

Not a little to his delight, the professor found that the

flying-machine would promptly answer his touch and will, rising easily off the ground, then descending at call, evidently having passed through the ordeal of the bygone evening without serious harm.

Still, all this consumed time, and it was after a late dinner that everything was pronounced in readiness for an ascension: the meat and fish nicely cooked and packed for carriage, a pot of strong coffee made and stowed beyond risk of leakage, the flying-machine itself quivering in that gentle breeze as though eager to find itself once more afloat far above the earth and its obstructions to easy navigation.

Waldo expressed some grief at leaving a spot where game came in such plentitude to find the hunter, and trout simply longed to be caught; but upon being assured of other opportunities, perhaps even more delightful, he sighed and gave consent to mount into space.

"Only - don't ask me to tackle any of those big dictionary fellows such as you talked about this morning, uncle Phaeton, for I simply can't; they'd get away with my baggage while I was trying to spell their names and title - and all that!"

Without any difficulty the aeromotor was sent out of and above the forest, heading towards the northwest; that is, direct for the heart of the Olympics, of whose marvels Professor Featherwit held such exalted hopes and expectations.

Grim and forbidding those mountains looked as the air-ship sailed swiftly over them, opening up a wider view when the bare, rugged crest was once left fairly to the rear. Save for those bald crowns, all below appeared a solid carpet of tree-tops, now lower, there higher, yet ever the same: seemingly impene-trable to man, should such an effort be made.

Once fairly within the charmed circle, leaving the rocky ridge behind, Professor Featherwit slackened speed, permitting the ship to drift onward at a moderate pace, one hand touching he steering-gear, while its fellow held a pair of field-glasses to his eager eyes.

All at once he gave a half-stifled cry, partly rising in his excitement, then crying aloud in thrilling tones:

"The sea, - an inland sea!"

JOSEPH E. BADGER, JR.

CHAPTER IX.

GRAPPLING A QUEER FISH.

At nearly the same moment both Bruno and Waldo caught a glimpse of water, shining clear and distinct amidst that sombre setting; but as yet a tree-crested elevation interfered with the prospect, and it was not until after the course of the air-ship had been materially changed, and some little time had elapsed, that aught definite could be determined as to the actual spread of that body of water.

This proved to be considerable, although it needed but a single look into the professor's face to learn that his eager hopes and exalted anticipations fell far short of realisation.

"Well, it's a sea all right," generously declared Waldo, giving a vigorous sniff by way of strengthening his words. "I can smell the salt clear from this. A sea, even if it isn't quite so large as others, - what one might term a lower-case c!"

If nothing else, that generous effort brought its reward in the dry little chuckle which escaped the professor's lips, and a kindly glow showed through his glasses as he turned towards Waldo with a nod of acknowledgment.

"Barring the salty scent, my dear boy, which probably finds birth in your kindly imagination. So, on the whole, perhaps 'twould be just as well to term it a lake."

"One of no mean dimensions, at any rate, uncle Phaeton."

"True, Bruno," with a nod of agreement, yet with forehead contracting into a network of troubled lines. "Naturally so, and yet - surely this must be merely a portion? Unless - yet I fail to see aught which might be interpreted as being -"

Promptly responding to each touch of hand upon steering-gear, the aeromotor swung smoothly around, sailing on even keel right into the teeth of the gentle wind, by this time near enough to that body of water for the air-voyagers to scan its surface: a considerable expanse, all told, yet by no means of such magnitude as Professor Featherwit had anticipated.

Too deeply absorbed in his own thoughts to notice the little cries and ejaculations which came from the brothers, he caused the aerostat to rise higher, slowly sweeping that extended field with his glasses.

He could see where several streams entered the body of water, coming from opposite points of the compass, and thus confirming at least one portion of his explained theory; but, so far as his visual powers went, there was no other considerable body of water to be discovered.

"Yet, how can that contracted basin contain all the drainage from this vast scope of country? How can we explain the stubborn fact of - What now, lads?"

An abrupt break, but one caused by the eager cry and loud speech from the lips of the younger Gillespie.

"Looky yonder! Isn't that one o' those sour-us dictionary fellows on a bender? Isn't that - but I don't - no, it's only -"

"Only a partly decayed tree gone afloat!" volunteered Bruno, with a merry laugh, as his eager brother drew back in evident chagrin.

"Well, that's all right. It ought to've been one, even if it isn't. What's the use in coming all this way, if we're not going to discover something beyond the common? And my sour-us is worth more than one of the other kind, after all; get it ashore and you might cook dinner for a solid month by it; now there!"

It was easily to be seen that Waldo had been giving free rein to his expectations ever since the professor's little lecture, but his natural chagrin was quickly forgotten in a matter of far greater interest.

Professor Featherwit had resumed his scrutiny of yonder body of water, slowly turning his glasses while holding the air-ship on a true course and even keel.

For a brief space nothing interfered with the steady motion of the field-glasses, but then something called for a more thorough examination, and little by little the savant leaned farther forward, breath coming more rapidly, face beginning to flush with deepening interest.

Bruno took note of all this, and, failing to see aught to account for the symptoms with unaided eyes, at length ventured to speak.

"What is it, uncle Phaeton? Something of interest, or your looks -"

Professor Featherwit gave a start, then lowered the glasses and reached them towards his nephew, speaking hurriedly:

"You try them, Bruno; your eyes are younger, and ought to be keener than mine. Yonder; towards the lower end of the - the lake, please."

Nothing loath, Gillespie complied, quickly finding the correct point upon which the professor's interest had centred, holding the glasses motionless for a brief space, then giving vent to an eager ejaculation.

"What is it all about, bless you, boy?" demanded Waldo, unable longer to curb his hot impatience. "Another drifting tree, eh?"

"No, but, - did you see it, uncle?"

"I saw something which - what do YOU see, first?"

"A great big suck, - a monster whirlpool which is hollowed like -"

"I knew it! I felt that must be the true solution of it all!" cried uncle Phaeton, squirming about pretty much as one might into whose veins had been injected quicksilver in place of ordinary blood. "The outlet! Where the surplus waters drain off to the Pacific Ocean!"

"I say, give me a chance, can't you?" interrupted Waldo, grasping the glasses and shifting his station for one more favourable as a lookout.

He had seen sufficient to catch the right angle, and then gave a suppressed snort as he took in the view. Half a minute thus, then a wild cry escaped his lips, closely followed by the words: "Now I DO see something! And it isn't a drifting tree, either! Or, that is, something else which - shove her closer, uncle Phaeton! True as you live, there's something caught in yonder big suck which is - closer, for love of glory!"

"If this is another joke, Waldo -"

"No, no, I tell you, Bruno! Shove her over, uncle, for, without this glass is hoodooed, we're needed right yonder, - and needed mighty bad, too!"

Little need of so much urging, by the way, since Professor Featherwit was but slightly less excited by their double discovery, and even before the glasses were clapped to Waldo's eyes the aerostat swung around to move at full speed towards that precise quarter of the compass.

"What is it you see, then, boy?" demanded Bruno, itching to take the glasses, yet straining his own vision towards that as yet far-distant spot.

"Something like - oh, see how the water is running out, - just like emptying a bathtub through a hole at the bottom! And see what - a man caught in the whirl, true's you're a foot high, uncle!"

"A man? Here? Impossible, - incredible, boy!" fairly exploded the professor, not yet ready to relinquish his cherished belief in a terra incognita.

The air-voyagers were swiftly nearing that point of interest, and now keen-eyed Bruno caught a glimpse of a drifting object which had been drawn within the influence of yonder whirlpool, but which was just as certainly a derelict from the forest.

"Another floating tree-trunk for Waldo!" he cried, with a short laugh, feeling far from unpleased that the intense strain upon his nerves should be thus lessened. "Try it again, lad, and perhaps -"

"Try your great-grandmother's cotton nightcap! Don't you suppose I can tell the difference between a tree and a -"

"Ranting, prancing, cavorting 'sour-us' right out of Webster's Unabridged, eh, laddy-buck?"

"That's all right, if you can only keep on thinking that way, old man; but if yonder isn't a fellow being in a mighty nasty pickle, then I wouldn't even begin to say so! And - you look, uncle Phaeton, please."

Nothing loath, the professor took the proffered glasses, and but an instant later he, too, gave a sharp cry of amazement, for he saw, clinging to the trunk of a floating tree, swiftly moving with those circling waters, a living being!

And but a few seconds later, Bruno made the same discovery, greatly to the delight of his younger brother.

"A man! And living, too!"

"Of course; reckon I'd make such a howl about a floater?" bluntly interjected Waldo. "But I'll do my crowing later on. For now we've got to get the poor fellow out of that, - just got to yank him
out!"

Through all this hasty interchange of words, the aeromotor was swiftly progressing, and now swung almost directly above the whirlpool, giving all a fair, unobstructed view of everything below.

The suction was so great that a sloping basin was formed, more than one hundred yards in diameter, while the actual centre lay a number of feet lower than the surrounding level.

Half-way down that perilous slope a great tree was revolving, and to this, as his forlorn hope, clung a half-clad man, plainly alive, since he was looking upward, and - yes, waving a hand and uttering a cry for aid and succour.

"Help! For love of God, save me!"

"White, - an American, too!" exploded Waldo, taking action as by brilliant inspiration. "Hang over him, uncle, for I'm going - to go fishing - for a man!"

Waldo was tugging at the grapnel and long drag-rope. Bruno was quick to divine his intention, and lent a deft hand, while the professor manipulated the helm so adroitly as to keep the flying-machine hovering directly above yonder imperilled stranger, leaning far over the hand-rail to shout downward:

"Have courage, sir, and stand ready to help yourself! We will rescue you if it lies within the possibilities of - we WILL save you!"

"You bet we just will, and right - like this," spluttered Waldo, as he cast the grapnel over the rail and swiftly lowered it by the rope. "Play you're a fish, stranger, and when you bite, hang on like grim death to a - steady, now!"

Fortunately nothing occurred to mar the programme so hastily arranged, for the drift was drawing nearer the centre of the whirl, and if once fairly caught by that, nothing human could preserve the stranger from death.

"Make a jump and grab it, if you can't do better!" cried Waldo, intensely excited now that the crisis was at hand.

The long rope with its iron weight swayed awkwardly in spite of all he could do to steady it, and as each one of the three prongs was meant for catching and holding fast to whatever they touched, there was no slight risk of impaling the man, thus giving him the choice of another and still more painful death.

Then, with a desperate grasp, a death-clutch, he caught one arm of the grapnel, holding fast as the shock came. He was carried clear of the tree, and partly submerged in the water as his added weight brought the flying-machine so much lower.

"Up, up, uncle Phaeton!" fairly howled Waldo, at the same time tugging at the now taut rope, in which he was ably seconded by his brother. "For love of - higher, uncle!"

Then the noble machine responded to the touch of its builder, lifting the dripping stranger clear of the whirling currents, swinging him away towards yonder higher level, where a fall would not prove so quickly fatal. And then the eager professor gave a shrill cheer as he saw the man, by a vigorous effort, draw his body upward sufficiently far to throw one leg over an arm of the grapnel itself.

Knowing now that the rescued was in no especial peril, uncle Phaeton left the air-ship to steer itself long enough for his nimble hands to take several turns of the drag-rope around the cleat provided for that express purpose, thus relieving both Bruno and Waldo of the heavy strain, which might soon begin to tell upon them.

"Hurrah for we, us, and company!" cried Waldo, relieving his lungs of a portion of their pent-up energy, then leaning perilously far over the edge of the machine to encourage the queer fish he had hooked.

JOSEPH E. BADGER, JR.

CHAPTER X.

RESCUED AND RESCUERS.

Despite their very natural excitement, caused by this peril and its foiling, Professor Featherwit retained nearly all his customary coolness and presence of mind.

Readily realising that after such a grim ordeal would almost certainly come a powerful revulsion, his first aim was to swing the stranger far enough away from the whirlpool to give him a fair chance for life, in case he should fall, through dizziness or physical collapse, from the end of the drag-rope.

This took but a few seconds, comparatively speaking, though, doubtless, each moment seemed an age to the rescued stranger. Then the professor slowed his ship, looking around in order to determine upon the wisest route to take.

For one thing, it would be severe work to draw the stranger bodily up and into the aerostat. For another, unless he should grow weak, or suffer from vertigo, both time and labour would be saved by taking him direct to the shore of this broad lake.

As soon as the rope was made fast, and the strain taken off their muscles as well as their minds, Bruno flashed a look around, naturally turning his eyes in the direction of the whirlpool.

Although less than a couple of minutes had elapsed since the man was lifted off the circling drift, even thus quickly had the end drawn nigh; for, even as he looked that way, Gillespie saw the great trunk sucked into the hidden sink, the top rising with a shiver clear out of the water as the butt lowered, a hollow, rumbling sound coming to all ears as -

"Gone!" cried Bruno, in awed tones, as the whole drift vanished from sight for ever.

"Sucked in by Jonah's whale, for ducats!" screamed Waldo, excitedly. "Fetch on your blessed 'sour-us' of both the male and female sect! Trot 'em to the fore, and if my little old suck don't take the starch out of their backbones, - they DID have backbones, didn't they, uncle Phaeton?"

Professor Featherwit frowned, and shook his head in silent reproof. More nearly, perhaps, than either of the boys, he realised what an awful peril this stranger had so narrowly escaped. It was far too early to turn that escape into jest, even for one naturally light of heart.

He leaned over the hand-rail, peering downward. He could see the rescued man sitting firmly in the bend of the grapnel, one hand tightly gripping the rope, its mate shading his eyes, as he stared fixedly towards the whirling death-pool, from whose jaws he had so miraculously been plucked.

There was naught of debility, either of body or of mind, to be read in that figure, and with his fears on that particular point set at rest, for the time being, Professor Featherwit called out, distinctly:

"Is it all well with you, my good friend? Can you hold fast until the shore is reached, think?"

"Heaven bless you, - yes!" came the reply, in half-choked tones. "If I fail in giving thanks -"

"Never mention it, friend; it cost us nothing," cheerily

interrupted the professor, then adding, "Hold fast, please, and we'll put on a wee bit more steam."

The flying-machine was now fairly headed for a strip of shore which offered an excellent opportunity for making a safe landing, and as that accelerated motion did not appear to materially affect the stranger, it took but a few minutes to clear the lake.

"Stand ready to let go when we come low enough, please," warned the professor, deftly managing his pet machine for that purpose.

The stranger easily landed, then watched the flying-machine with painfully eager gaze, hands clasped almost as though in prayer. A more remarkable sight than this half-naked shape, burned brown by the sun, poorly protected by light skins, with sinew fastenings, could scarcely be imagined; and there was something close akin to tears in more eyes than one when he came running in chase, arms outstretched, and voice wildly appealing:

"Oh, come back! Take me, - don't leave me, - for love of God and humanity, don't leave me to this living death!"

Professor Featherwit called back a hasty assurance, and brought the air-ship to a landing with greater haste than was exactly prudent, all things considered; but who could keep cool blood and unmoved heart, with yonder piteous object before their eyes?

When he saw that the flying-machine had fairly landed, and beheld its inmates stepping forth upon the sands with friendly salutations, the rescued stranger staggered, hands clasping his temples for a moment of drunken reeling, then he fell forward like one smitten by the hand of sudden death.

Professor Featherwit called out a few curt directions, which were promptly obeyed by his nephews, and after a few minutes' well-directed work consciousness was restored, and the stranger feebly strove to give them thanks.

In vain these were set aside. He seemed like one half-insane from joy, and none who saw and heard could think that all this emotion arose from the simple rescue from the whirlpool. Nor did it.

Wildly, far from coherently, the poor fellow spoke, yet something of the awful truth was to be gleaned even from those broken, disjointed sentences.

For ten years an exile in these horrible wilds. For ten years not a single glimpse of white face or figure. For ten ages no intelligible voice, save his own; and that, through long disuse, had threatened to desert him!

"Ten years!" echoed Waldo, in amazement. "Why didn't you rack out o' this, then? I know I would; even if the woods were full of - 'sour-us' and the like o' that! Yes, SIR!"

A low, husky laugh came through those heavily bearded lips, and the stranger flung out his hands in a sweeping gesture, sunken eyes glowing with an almost savage light as he spoke with more coherence:

"Why is it, young gentleman? Why did I not leave, do you ask? Look! All about you it stretches: a cell, - a death-cell, from which escape is impossible! Here I have fought for what is ever more precious than bare life: for liberty; but though ten awful years have rolled by, here I remain, in worse than prison! Escape? Ah, how often have I attempted to escape, only to fail, because escape from these wilds is beyond the power of any person not gifted with wings!"

"Ten years, you say, good friend? And all that time you have lived here alone?" asked the professor, curiously.

"Ten years, - ten thousand years, I could almost swear, only for keeping the record so carefully, so religiously. And - pitiful Lord! How gladly would I have given my good right arm, just for one faraway glimpse of civilisation! How often - but I am wearying you, gentlemen, and you may - pray don't think that I am crazy; you will not?"

Both the professor and Bruno assured him to the contrary, but Waldo was less affected, and his curiosity could no longer be kept within bounds. Gently tapping one hairy arm, he spoke:

"I say, friend, what were you doing out yonder in the big suck? Didn't you know the fun was hardly equal to the risk, sir?"

"Easy, lad," reproved the professor; but with a a smile, which strangely softened that haggard, weather-worn visage, the stranger spoke:

"Nay, kind sir, do not check the young gentleman. If you could only realise how sweet it is to my poor ears, - the sound of a friendly voice! For so many weary years I have never heard one word from human lips which I could understand or make answer to. And now, - what is it you wish to know, my dear boy?"

"Well, since you've lived here so long, surely you hadn't ought to get caught in such a nasty pickle; unless it was through accident?"

"It was partly accidental. One that would have cost me dearly had not you come to my aid so opportunely. And yet, - only for one thing, I could scarcely have regretted vanishing for ever down that suck!"

His voice choked, his head bowed, his hands came together in a nervous grip, all betokening unusual agitation. Even Waldo was just a bit awed, and the stranger was first to break that silence with words.

"How did the mishap come about, is it, young gentleman?" he said, a wan smile creeping into his face, and relaxing those tensely drawn muscles once more. "While I was trying to replenish my stock of provisions, and after this fashion, good friends.

"I was fishing from a small canoe, and as the bait was not taken well, I must have fallen into a day dream, thinking of - no matter, now. And during that dreaming, the breeze must have blown me well out into the lake, for when I was roused up by a sharp jerk at my line, I found myself near its middle, without knowing just how I came there.

"I have no idea what sort of fish had taken my bait, - there are many enormous ones in the lake, - but it proved far too powerful for me to manage, and dragged the canoe swiftly through the water, heading directly for the outlet, yonder."

"Why didn't you let it go free, then?"

"The line was fastened to the prow, and I could not loosen it in time. I drew my knife, - one of flint, but keen enough to serve, - only to have it jerked out of my hand and into the water. Then, just as the fish must have plunged into the suck, I abandoned my canoe, jumping overboard."

"That's just what I was wondering about," declared Waldo, with a vigorous nod of his head. "Yet we found you - there?"

"Because I am a wretchedly poor swimmer. I managed to reach a drift which had not yet fairly entered the whirl, but I could do nothing more towards saving myself. Then - you can guess the rest, gentlemen."

"And the canoe?" demanded Waldo, content only when all points were made manifest.

"I saw it dragged down the centre of the suck," with an involuntary shiver. "The fish must have plunged into the underground river, whether willingly or not I can only surmise. But all the while I was drifting yonder, around and around, with each circuit drawing closer to the awful end, I could not help picturing to myself how the canoe must have plunged down, and down, and - burr-r-r!"

A shuddering shiver which was more eloquent than words; but Waldo was not yet wholly content, finding an absorbing interest in that particular subject.

"You call it a river: how do you know it's a river?"

"Of course, I can only guess at the facts, my dear boy," the stranger made reply, smiling once more, and, with an almost timid gesture, extending one hairy paw to lightly touch and gently stroke the arm nearest him.

Bruno turned away abruptly, for that gesture, so simple in itself, yet so full of pathos to one who bore in mind those long years of solitary exile, brought a moisture to his big brown eyes of which, boy-like, he felt ashamed.

Professor Featherwit likewise took note, and with greater presence of mind came to the rescue, lightly resting a hand upon the stranger's half-bare shoulder while addressing his words to the youngster.

A tremulous sigh escaped those bearded lips, and their owner drew closer to the wiry little aeronaut, plainly drawing great comfort from that mere contact. And with like ease uncle Phaeton lifted one of those hairy arms to rest it over his own shoulders, speaking briskly the while.

"There is only one way of demonstrating the truth more clearly, my youthful inquisitor, and that is by sending you on a voyage of exploration. Are you willing to make the attempt, Waldo?"

"Not this evening; some other evening, - maybe!" drawing back a bit, with a shake of his curly pate to match. "But, I say, uncle Phaeton -"

"Allow me to complete my say, first, dear boy," with a bland smile. "That is easily done, though, for it merely consists of this: yonder sink, or whirlpool, is certainly the method this lake has of relieving itself of all surplus water. Everything points to a subterranean river which connects this lake with the Pacific Ocean."

"Wonder how long I'd have to hold my breath to make the trip?"

CHAPTER XI.

ANOTHER SURPRISE FOR THE PROFESSOR.

The stranger laughed aloud at this, then seemed surprised that aught of mirth could be awakened where grief and despair had so long reigned supreme.

"You will come with me to - to my den, gentlemen?" he asked, still nervous, and plainly loath to do aught which indicated a return to his recent dreary method of living.

"Is the distance great?" asked Professor Featherwit, with a glance towards the aeromotor, then flashing his gaze further, as though to guard against possible harm coming to that valuable piece of property.

More than ever to be guarded now, since the words spoken by this exile. Better death in yonder mighty whirlpool than a half-score years' imprisonment here!

Not so very far, he was assured, while it would be comparatively easy to float the air-ship above the trees, there of no extraordinary growth.

At the same time this assurance was given, the stranger could not mask his uneasiness of mind, and it was really pitiful to see one so strong in body and limb, so weak otherwise.

But uncle Phaeton was a fairly keen judge of human nature,

and possessed no small degree of tact. Divining the real cause of that dread, he took the easiest method of allaying it, speaking briskly as he moved across to the aerostat.

"Bear the gentleman company, my lads, while I manage the ship. You will know what signals to make, and I can contrive the rest."

Again the recluse laughed, but now it was through pure joy, such as he had not experienced for long years gone by. He was not to be deserted by his rescuers from the whirlpool, and that was comfort enough for the moment.

Thanks to that guidance, but little time was cut to waste, Professor Featherwit taking the flying-machine away from the shore of the lake, floating slowly above the tree-tops, guiding his movements by those below, finally effecting a safe landing in a miniature glade, at no great distance from the "den" alluded to by their new-found friend.

"It will be perfectly safe here," the exile hastened to give assurance, as that landing was made. "Then, too, this is the only spot nigh at hand from which a hasty ascent could well be made, even with such an admirable machine as yours. Ah, me!" with a long breath which lacked but little of being a sigh, as he keenly, eagerly examined the aerostat. "A marvel! Who would have dared predict such another, only a dozen years ago? I thought we had drawn very close to perfection while I was in the profession, but this, - marvellous!"

Both words and manner gave the keen-witted professor a clew to one mystery, and he quickly spoke:

"Then you were familiar with aerostatics, sir? Your name is -"

"Edgecombe, - Cooper Edgecombe."

"What?" with undisguised surprise in face as in voice.

"Professor Edgecombe, the celebrated balloonist who was lost so long ago?"

"Ay! lost here in this thrice accursed wilderness!" passionately cried the exile; then, as though abashed by his own outburst, he turned away, pausing again only when at the entrance to his dreary refuge of many years.

"Give the poor fellow his own way until he has had time to rally, boys," muttered uncle Phaeton, in lowered tones, before following that lead. "I can understand it better, now, and this is - still is the terra incognita of which I have dreamed so long!"

That refuge proved to be a large, fairly dry cavern, the entrance to which was admirably masked by vines and creepers, while the stony soil just there retained no trace of footprints to tell dangerous tales.

Mr. Edgecombe vanished, but not for long. Then, showing a light, formed of fat and twisted wick in a hollowed bit of hardwood, he begged his rescuers to enter.

No second invitation was needed, for even the professor felt a powerful curiosity to learn what method had been followed by this enforced exile; how he had managed to live for so many weary years.

With only that smoky lamp to shed light around the place, critical investigation was a matter of time and painstaking, although a general idea of the cavern was readily formed.

High overhead arched the rocky roof, blackened by smoke, and looking more gloomy than nature had intended. The side walls were likewise irregular, now showing tiny niches and nooks, then jutting out to form awkward points and elbows, which were but partially disguised by such articles of wear and daily use as the exile had collected during the years gone by, or since his occupancy first began.

So much the professor took in with his initial glances, but then he left Waldo and his brother to look more closely, himself giving thought to the being whom they had so happily saved from the whirlpool.

"Professor Edgecombe!" he again exclaimed, grasping those roughened hands to press them cordially. "I ought to have recognised you at sight, no doubt, since I have watched your ascents time and time again."

The exile smiled faintly, shaking his head and giving another sigh.

"Ah, me! 'twas vastly different, then. I only marvel that you should give me credit when I lay claim to that name, so long – it has long faded from the public's memory, sir."

But uncle Phaeton shook his head, decidedly.

"No, no, I assure you, my friend; far from it. Whenever the topic is brought to the front; whenever aerostatics are discussed, your name and fame are sure to play a prominent part. And yet, - you disappeared so long ago, never being heard of after -"

"After sailing away upon the storm for which I had waited and prayed, for so many weary, heart-sick months!"

"So the rumour ran, but we all believed that must be an exaggeration, and not for a long time was all hope abandoned. Then, more hearts than one felt sore and sad at thoughts of your untimely fate."

"A fate infinitely worse than ordinary death such as was credited me," huskily muttered the exile. "Ten years, - and ever since I have been here, helpless to extricate myself, doomed to a living death, which none other can ever fully realise! Doomed to - to -"

His voice choked, and he turned away to hide his emotions.

Professor Featherwit thoroughly appreciated the interruption which came through Waldo's lips just at that moment.

"Oh, I say, - uncle Phaeton!"

"What is it, lad? Don't meddle with what doesn't -"

"Looking can't hurt, can it? And to think people ever got along with such things as these!"

Waldo was squared before sundry articles depending from the side wall, and as the professor drew closer, he, too, displayed a degree of interest which was really remarkable.

A gaily colored tunic of thickly quilted cotton was hanging beside an oddly shaped war club, the heavier end of which was armed with blades of stone which gleamed and sparkled even in that dim light. And attached to this weapon was another, hardly less curious: a knife formed of copper, with heft and blade all from one piece of metal.

"Here is the rest of the outfit," said Edgecombe, holding forth a bow and several feathered arrows with obsidian heads.

Professor Featherwit gave a low, eager cry as he handled the various articles, both face and manner betraying intense delight, which found partial vent in words a little later.

"Wonderful! Marvellous! Superb! I envy you, sir; I can't help but envy your possession of so magnificent - and so well-preserved, too! That is the marvel of marvels!"

"Well, to be sure, I haven't used them very much. The bow and arrows I could manage fairly well, after busy practice. They have saved me from more than one hungry night. But as for the rest -"

"You might have worn the - Is it a ghost-dance shirt, though?" hesitatingly asked Waldo, gingerly fingering the wadded tunic.

"Waldo, I'm ashamed of you, boy!" almost harshly reproved the professor. "Ghost-dance shirt, indeed! And this one of the most complete - the only perfectly preserved specimen of the ancient Aztec - pray, my good friend, where did you discover them? Surely there can be no burial mounds so far above the latitude where that unfortunate race lived and died?"

Mr. Edgecombe shook his head, with a puzzled look, then made reply:

"No, sir. I took these all from an Indian I was forced to kill in order to save my own life. I never thought - You are ill, sir?"

"Bless my soul!" ejaculated the professor, falling back a pace or two, then sitting down with greater force than grace, all the while gazing upon those weapons like one in a daze. "Found them - Indian - killed him in order to - bless my soul!"

Then, with marvellous activity for one of his age, the professor recovered his footing, mumbling something about tripping a heel, then resumed his examination of the curiosities as though he had care for naught beside.

Cooper Edgecombe turned away, and the professor improved the opportunity by muttering to the brothers:

"Careful, lads. Give the poor fellow his own way in all things, for he is - he surely must be - eh?"

Forefinger covertly tapped forehead, for there was no time granted for further explanations. Edgecombe turned again, speaking in hard, even strained tones:

"Fifteen years ago this month, on the 27th, to be exact, a balloon with two passengers was carried away on a terrific gale of wind which blew from the southeast. This happened in

Washington Territory. Can you tell me - has anything ever been heard of either balloon or its inmates?"

Professor Featherwit shook his head in negation before saying:

"Not to my knowledge, though doubtless the prints of the day -"

Cooper Edgecombe shook both head and hand with strange impatience.

"No, no. I know they were never heard from up to ten years ago, but since then - I am a fool to even dream of such a thing, and yet, - only for that faint hope I would have gone mad long ago!"

Indeed, he looked little less than insane as it was.

CHAPTER XII.

THE STORY OF A BROKEN LIFE.

This was the idea that occurred to both uncle and nephews, but they had seen and heard enough to excuse all that, and Professor Featherwit spoke again, in mildly curious tones:

"Sorry I am unable to give you better tidings, my good friend, but, so far as my knowledge extends, nothing has come to light of recent years. And - if not a leading question - were those passengers friends of your own?"

"Only - merely my - my wife and little daughter," came the totally unexpected reply, followed by a forced laugh which sounded anything but mirthful.

Uncle Phaeton, intensely chagrined, hastened to apologise for his luckless break, but Cooper Edgecombe cut him short, asking that the matter be let drop for the time being.

"I will talk; I feel that I must tell you all, or lose what few wits I have left," he declared, huskily. "But not right now. It is growing late. You must be hungry. I have no very extensive larder, but with my little will go the gratitude of a man who -"

His voice choked, and he left the sentence unfinished, hurrying away to prepare such a meal as his limited means would permit.

JOSEPH E. BADGER, JR.

While Edgecombe was kindling a fire in one corner of the cavern, opening a pile of ashes to extract the few carefully cherished coals by means of which the wood was to be fired, uncle and one nephew left the den to look after the flying-machine and contents.

Bruno remained behind, in obedience to a hint from the professor, lest the exile should dread desertion, after all.

"Take these in and open them, Waldo," said the professor, selecting several cans from the stock in the locker. "Poor fellow! 'Twill be like a foretaste of civilisation, just to see and smell, much less taste, the fruit."

"Even if he has turned looney, eh, uncle Phaeton?"

"Careful, boy! I hardly think he is just that far gone; but, even if so, what marvel? Think of all he must have suffered during so many long, dreary years! and - his wife and child! I wonder - I do wonder if he really killed - but that is incredible, simply and utterly incredible! An Aztec - here - alive!"

"Dead, uncle Phaeton," corrected Waldo. "Killed the redskin, he said, and I really reckon he meant it. Why not, pray?"

"But - an Aztec, boy!" exclaimed the bewildered savant, unable to pass that point. "The tunic of quilted cotton, the escaupil! The maquahuitl, with its blades of grass! The bow and arrows which - all, all surely of Aztecan manufacture, yet seemingly fresh and serviceable as though in use but a month ago! And the race extinct for centuries!"

"Well, unless he's a howling liar from 'way up the crick, he extincted one of 'em," cheerfully commented Waldo, bearing his canned fruit to the cavern.

Professor Featherwit followed shortly after, finding the exile busy preparing food, looking and acting far more naturally than he had since his rescue from the whirlpool. And then, until the evening meal was announced, uncle Phaeton hovered near those amazing curiosities, now gazing like one in a waking dream, then gingerly fingering each article in turn, as though hoping to find a solution for his enigma through the sense of touch.

Taken all in all, that was far from a pleasant or enjoyable meal. A sense of restraint rested upon each one of that little company, and not one succeeded in fairly breaking it away, though each tried in turn.

Despite the struggle made by the exile to hold all emotions well under subjection, Cooper Edgecombe failed to hide his almost childish delight at sight and taste of those canned goods, and it did not require much urging on the part of his rescuers to ensure his partaking freely.

But the cap-sheaf came when uncle Phaeton, true to his habit of long years, after eating, produced pipe and pouch, the fragrant tobacco catching the exile's nostrils and drawing a low, tremulous cry from his lips.

No need to ask what was the matter, for that eager gaze, those quivering fingers, were enough. And just as though this had been his express purpose, the professor passed the pipe over, quietly speaking:

"Perhaps you would like a little smoke after your supper, my good friend? Oblige me by -"

"May I? Oh, sir, may I - really taste - oh, oh, oh!"

Bruno struck a match and steadied the pipe until the tobacco was fairly ignited, then drew back and left the exile to himself for the time being. And, as covert glances told them, never before had their eyes rested upon mortal being so intensely happy as was the long-lost aeronaut then and there.

At a sign from the professor, Bruno and Waldo silently arose and left the cavern, bearing their guardian company to where the air-ship was resting. And there they busied themselves with making preparations for the night, which was just settling over that portion of the earth.

Presently Cooper Edgecombe appeared, the empty pipe in hand, held as one might caress an inestimable treasure, a dreamy, almost blissful expression upon his sun-browned face.

"I thank you, sir, more than tongue can tell," he said, quietly, as he restored the pipe to its owner. "If you could only realise what I have suffered through this deprivation! I, an inveterate smoker; yet suddenly deprived of it, and so kept for ten long years! If I had had a pipe and tobacco, I believe - but enough."

"I can sympathise with you, at least in part, my friend. Will you have another smoke, by the way?"

"No, no, not now; I feel blessed for the moment, and more might be worse than none, after so long deprivation. And - may I talk openly to you, dear, kind friends? May I tell you - am I selfish in wishing to trouble you thus? Ten years, remember, and not a soul to speak with!"

He laughed, but it was a sorry mirth; and not caring to trust his tongue just then, uncle Phaeton nodded his head emphatically while filling his pipe for himself. But Waldo never lacked for words, and spoke out:

"That's all right, sir; we can listen as long as you can chin-chin. Tell us all about - well, what's the matter with that big Injun?"

"Quiet, Waldo. Say what best pleases you, my friend. You can be sure of one thing, - sympathetic listeners, if nothing better."

With a curious shiver, as though afflicted with a sudden chill, Edgecombe turned partly away, figure drawn rigidly erect, hands tightly clasped behind his back. A brief silence, then he spoke in tones of forced composure.

"A balloon was the best, in my day, and I was proud of my profession, although even then I was dreaming of better things - of something akin to this marvellous creation of yours, sir," casting a fleeting glance at the air-ship, then at the face of its builder, afterward resuming his former attitude.

"Let that pass, though. I wanted to tell you how I met with my awful loss; how I came to be out here in this modern hell!

"I had a wife, a daughter, each of whom felt almost as powerful an interest in aerostatics as I did myself. And one day - but, wait!

"I had an enemy, too; one who had, years before, sought to win my love for his own; in vain, the cur! And that day - we were out here in Washington Territory, living in comparative solitude that I might the better study out the theory I was slowly shaping in my brain.

"The day was beautiful, but almost oppressively warm, and, as they so frequently wished, I let my dear ones up in the balloon, securely fastening it below. And then - God forgive me! - I went back to town for something; I forget just what, now.

"A sudden storm came up. I hurried homeward; home to me was wherever my dear ones chanced to be; but I was just too late! That devil of all devils was ahead of me, and I saw him - merciful God! I saw him - cut the ropes and let the balloon dart away upon that awful gale!"

His voice choked, and for a few minutes silence reigned. Knowing how vain must be any attempt to offer consolation, the trio of air-voyagers said nothing, and presently Cooper Edgecombe spoke.

"I killed the demon. I nearly tore him limb from limb; I would have done just that, only for those who came hurrying after me from town, knowing that I might need help in bringing my balloon to earth in safety. They dragged me away, but 'twas too late to cheat my miserable vengeance. That hound was dead, but - my darlings were gone, for ever!"

Another pause, then quieter, more coherent speech.

"God alone knows whither my wife and child were taken. The general drift was in this direction, but how far they were carried, or how long they may have lived, I can only guess; enough that, despite all my inquiries, made far and wide in every direction, I never heard aught of either balloon or passengers!

"After that, I had but one object in life: to follow along the track of that storm, and either find my loved ones, or - or some clew which should for ever solve my awful doubts! And for two long years or more I fought to pierce these horrid fastnesses, - all in vain. No mortal man could succeed, even when urged on by such a motive as mine.

"Then I determined upon another course. I worked and slaved until I could procure another balloon, as nearly like the one I lost as might be constructed. Then I watched and waited for just such another storm as the one upon whose wings my darlings were borne away, meaning to take the same course, and so find -"

"Why, man, dear, you must have been insane!" impulsively cried the professor, unable longer to control his tongue.

"Perhaps I was; little wonder if so," admitted Edgecombe, turning that way, with a wan smile lighting up his visage. "I could no longer reason. I could only act. I had but that one grim hope, to eventually discover what time and exposure to the weather might have left of my lost loves.

"Then, after so long waiting, the storm came, blowing in the same direction as that other. I cut my balloon loose, and let it drift. I looked and waited, hoping, longing, yet - failing! I was wrecked, here in this wilderness. My balloon was carried away.

I failed to find - aught!"

Cooper Edgecombe turned towards the air-ship, with a sigh of regret.

"If one had something like this then, I might have found them, - even alive! But now - too late - eternally too late!"

CHAPTER XIII.

THE LOST CITY OF THE AZTECS.

Uncle Phaeton was more than willing to do the honours of his pet invention, and this afforded a most happy diversion, although the deepening twilight hindered any very extensive examination.

Cooper Edgecombe showed himself in a vastly different light while thus engaged, his shrewd questions, his apt comments, quite effectually removing the far from agreeable doubts born of his earlier words and demeanour.

"Well, if he's looney, it's only on some points, not as the whole porker, anyway," confidentially asserted Waldo, when an opportunity offered. "Coax him to tell how he knocked the redskin out, uncle Phaeton."

Little need of recalling that perplexing incident to the worthy savant, for, try as he might, Featherwit could not keep from brooding over that wondrous collection of relics pertaining to a long-since extinct people. Of course, the last one had perished ages ago; and yet - and yet -

Through his half-bewildered brain flashed the accounts given by the coast tribes, members of which he had so frequently interviewed concerning this unknown land, one and all of whom had more or less to say in regard to a strange people, terrible fighters, mighty hunters, one burning glance from whose eyes carried death and decay unto all who were foolhardy enough even to attempt to pass those mighty barriers, built up by a beneficent nature. Only for that nearly impassable wall, the entire earth would be overrun and dominated by these monsters in human guise.

Then, after the air-ship was cared for to the best of his ability, and the night-guard set in place so that an alarm might give warning of any illegal intrusion, the little party returned to the cavern home of the exile where, after another refusal on his part, the professor filled and lighted his beloved pipe.

Almost in spite of himself Featherwit was drawn towards those marvellous articles depending from the wall, and, as he gazed in silent marvel, Cooper Edgecombe drew nigh, with still other articles to complete the collection.

"You may possibly find something of interest in these, too, dear sir, although I have given them rather rough usage. This formed a rather comfortable cap, and -"

"A helmet! And sandals! A sash which is - yes! worn about the waist, mainly to support weapons, and termed a maxtlatl, which - and all sufficiently well preserved to be readily recognised as genuine - unless - Surely I am dreaming!"

If not precisely that, the worthy professor assuredly was almost beside himself while examining these articles of warrior's wear, one by one, knowing that neither eyes nor memory were at fault, yet still unable to believe those very senses.

Up to this, Cooper Edgecombe had felt but a passing interest in the matter, forming as it did but a single incident in a more than ordinarily eventful life; but now he began to divine at least a portion of the truth, and his face was lighted up with unusual animation, when Phaeton Featherwit turned that way, to almost sharply demand:

"Where did you gain possession of these weapons and

garments, sir? And how, - from whom?"

"I took them from an Indian, nearly two years ago. He caught me off my guard, and, when I saw that I could neither hide nor flee, I fought for my life," explained the exile; then giving a short, bitter laugh, to add: "Strange, is it not? Although I had long since grown weary of existence such as this, I fought for it; I turned wild beast, as it were! Then, after all was over, I took these things, more because I feared his comrades might suspect -"

"His comrades?" echoed the professor. "More than the one, then? You killed him, but - there were others, still?"

"Many of them; far too many for any one man to withstand," earnestly declared the exile. "I made all haste in bearing the redskin here, obliterating all signs as quickly as possible; yet for days and nights I cowered here in utter darkness, each minute expecting an attack from too powerful a force for standing against."

Uncle Phaeton rubbed his hands briskly, shifting his weight hurriedly from one foot to its mate, then back again, the very personification of eager interest and growing conviction.

"More of them? A strong force? Armed, - and garbed as of old? The clothing, the footwear, and, above all else, the weapons, purely Aztecan? And here, only two short years ago?"

"Sadly long and hideously dreary years I have found them, sir," the exile said, in dejected tones.

The professor burst into a shrill, excited laugh, which sounded almost hysterical, and, not a little to the amazement of his nephews, broke into a regular dance, jigging it right merrily, hands on hips, head perked, and chin in air, at the same time striving to carry the tune in his far from melodious voice.

After all, perhaps no better method could have been taken to work off his almost hysterical excitement, and presently he paused, panting and heated, chuckling after an abashed fashion as he encountered the eyes of his nephews.

"Not a word, my dear boys," he hastened to plead. "I had to do something or - or explode! I feel better, now. I can behave myself, I hope. I am calm, cool, and composed as - the genuine Aztecs! And we are the ones to discover that - oh, I forgot!"

For Waldo was fairly exploding with mirth, while Bruno smiled, and even the exile appeared to be amused to a certain extent at his expense.

Little by little, the worthy savant calmed down, and then, almost forcing the exile to indulge in another delicious smoke, he led up to the subject in which his interest was fairly intense.

Cooper Edgecombe was willing enough to tell all that lay in his power, although he was only beginning to realise how much that might mean to the world at large, judging by the actions of the professor.

According to his account, the great lake, or drainage reservoir of the Olympics, was a sort of semi-yearly rendezvous for a warlike tribe of red men, where they congregated for the purpose of catching and drying vast quantities of fish, doubtless to be used during the winter.

"As a general thing they pitch their camp on the other side, over towards the northeast; but small parties are pretty sure to rove far and wide, coming around this way quite as often as not."

"And their garb, - the weapons they bore?" asked the professor.

Edgecombe motioned towards those articles in which such a lively interest had been awakened, then said that, while few of the red men who had come beneath his near observation had been so elaborately equipped, he had taken notice of similar weapons and garments, with additions which he strove hard to describe with accuracy.

Nearly every sentence which crossed his lips served to confirm the marvellous truth which had so dazzlingly burst upon the professor's eager brain, and with a glib tongue he named each weapon, each garment, as accurately as ever set down in ancient history, not a little to the wide-eyed amazement of Waldo Gillespie.

"Worse than those blessed 'sour-us' and cousins," he confided to his brother, in a whisper. "Reckon it's all right, Bruno? Uncle isn't - eh?"

But uncle Phaeton paid them no attention, so deeply was he stirred by this wondrous revelation. He felt that he was upon the verge of a discovery which would startle the wide world as no recent announcement had been able to do, unless - but it surely must be correct!

And then, when Cooper Edgecombe finished all he could tell concerning those queerly armed and gaudily garbed red men, the professor let loose his tongue, telling what glorious hopes and dazzling anticipations were now within him.

"For hundreds upon hundreds of years there have been wild, weird legends about the Lost City, but that merely meant a mass of wondrous ruins, long since overwhelmed by shifting sands, somewhere in the heart of the great American desert, so-called.

"By some it was claimed that this ancient city owed its primal existence to a fragment of the Aztecs, driven from their native quarters in Old Mexico. By others 'twas attributed unto one of the fabulous 'Lost Tribes of Israel,' but even the most enthusiastic never for one moment dreamed of - this!"

"Except yourself, uncle Phaeton," cut in Waldo, with a subdued grin. "This must be one of the marvels you calculated on discovering, thanks to the flying-machine, eh?"

"Nay, my boy; I never let my imagination soar half so high as all that," quickly answered the professor. "But now - now I feel confident that just such a discovery lies before us, and with the dawn of a new day we will ascend and look for the glorious 'Lost City of the Aztecs!' "

Again the savant sprang to his feet, wildly gesticulating as he strode to and fro, striving to thus work off some of the intense excitement which had taken full possession. And words fell rapidly from his lips the while, only a portion of which need be placed upon record in this connection, however.

"A fico for the paltry lost cities of musty tradition, now! They may sleep beneath the sand-storms of countless years, but this - I would gladly give one of my eyes for the certainty that its mate might gaze upon such a wondrous spectacle as - Oh, if it might only prove true! If I might only discover such a stupendous treasure! Aztecs! And in the present day! Alive - armed and garbed as of yore! Amazing! Incredible! Astounding beyond the wildest dreams of a confirmed -"

With startling swiftness uncle Phaeton wheeled to confront the exile, gripping his arm with fierce vigour, as he shrilly demanded:

"Opium - are you an eater of drugs, Cooper Edgecombe?"

Even as the words crossed his lips, the professor realised how preposterous they must sound, but the exile shook his head, earnestly.

"I never ate drugs in that shape, sir. Even if I had been addicted to morphine and the like, how could I indulge the appetite here, in these gloomy, lonely wilds?"

"I beg your pardon, sir; most humbly I implore your forgiveness. I have but one excuse - this wondrous - Good

JOSEPH E. BADGER, JR.

night! I'm going to bed before I add to my new reputation as - a blessed idiot, no less!"

CHAPTER XIV.

A MARVELLOUS VISION.

But the night was considerably older ere any one of that quartette lost himself in slumber, for all had been too thoroughly wrought up by the exciting events of the past day for sleep to claim an easy subject.

By common consent, however, that one particular subject was barred for the present, and then, sitting in a cosy group about the glowing fire there in the cavern, the recently formed friends talked and chatted, asking and answering questions almost past counting.

Little wonder that such should be the case, so far as Cooper Edgecombe was concerned, since he had been lost to the busy world and its many changes for a long decade.

Then, too, his own dreary existence held a strange charm for the air-voyagers, and the exile grew wonderfully cheerful and bright-eyed as he in part depicted his struggles to sustain life against such heavy odds, and still strove to keep alive that one hope, - that even yet he might be able to discover a clew to his loved and lost ones.

"Not alive; I have long since abandoned that faint hope. But if I might only find something to make sure, something that I could pray over, then bury where my heart could hover above -"

JOSEPH E. BADGER, JR.

"You are still alive, good friend, yet you have spent long years out here in the wilderness," gently suggested the professor.

Edgecombe flinched, as one might when a rude hand touches a still raw wound.

"But they, my wife, my baby girl, - they could never have lived as I have existed. They surely must have perished; if not at once, then when the first cruel storms of hideous winter came howling down from the far north!"

"Unless they were found and rescued by - who knows, my good sir?" forcing a cheerful smile, which, unfortunately, was only surface-born, as the exile lifted his head with a start and a gasping ejaculation. "Since it seems fairly well proven that this supposedly unknown land is actually inhabited, why may your loved ones not have been rescued?"

"The Indians? You mean by the Aztecs, sir?"

"If Aztecans they should really prove; why not?"

"But, surely I have heard - sacrifices?" huskily breathed the greatly agitated man, while the professor, realising how he was making a bad matter worse, brazenly falsified the records, declaring that no human sacrifices had ever stained the record of that noble, honourable, gallant race; and then changed the subject as quickly as might be.

Nevertheless, there was one good effect following that talk. Cooper Edgecombe had dreaded nothing so much as the fear of being left behind by these, the first white people he had seen for what seemed more than an ordinary lifetime; but now, when the professor hinted at a longing to take a spin through ether, for the purpose of winning a wider view, he eagerly seconded that idea, even while realising that it would be difficult to take him along with the rest.

Still, nothing was definitely settled that evening, and at a fairly respectable hour before the turn of night, the air-voyagers were wrapped in their blankets and soundly slumbering.

Not so the exile. Sleep was far from his brain, and while he really knew that danger could hardly menace that wondrous bit of ingenious mechanism, he watched it throughout that long night, ready to risk his own life in its defence should the occasion arise.

Why not, since his whole future depended upon the aeromotor? By its aid he hoped to reach civilization once more; and in spite of the great loss which had wrecked his life, he was thrilled to the centre by that glorious prospect. Here he was dead while breathing; there he would at least be in touch with his fellow men once more!

An early meal was prepared by the exile, and in readiness when his trio of guests awakened to the new day; and then, while busily discussing the really appetising viands placed before them, the next move was fully determined upon.

Not a little to his secret delight, the professor heard Edgecombe broach the subject of further explorations, and seeing that his excitement had passed away in goodly measure during the silent watches of the night, he talked with greater freedom.

"Of course we'll keep in touch with you, here, friend, and take no decisive move without your knowledge and consent. Our fate shall be yours, and your fate shall be ours. Only - I would dearly love to catch a glimpse of - If there should actually be a Lost City in existence!"

"If there is, as there surely must be one of some description, judging from the number of red men I have seen collecting here at the lake," observed the exile, "you certainly ought to make the discovery with the aid of your air-ship. You can ascend at will, of course, sir?"

Nothing loath, the professor spoke of his pet and its wondrous capabilities, and then all hands left the cavern for the outer air, to prepare for action.

As a further assurance, uncle Phaeton begged Edgecombe to enter the aerostat, then skilfully caused the vessel to float upward into clear space, sailing out over the lake even to the whirlpool itself before turning, his passenger eagerly watching every move and touch of hand, asking questions which proved him both shrewd and ingenious, from a mechanical point of view.

Returning to their starting-point, Edgecombe sprang lightly to earth to make way for the brothers, face ruddy and eyes aglow as he again begged them all to keep watch for aught which might solve the mystery yet surrounding the fate of his loved ones.

The promise was given, together with an earnest assurance that they would soon return; then the parting was cut as short as might be, all feeling that such a course was wisest and kindest, after all.

For an hour or more the air-ship sped on, high in air, its inmates viewing the various and varying landmarks beneath and beyond them, all marvelling at the fact that such an immense scope of country should for so long be left in its native virginity, especially where all are so land-hungry.

Then, as nothing of especial interest was brought to their notice, uncle Phaeton quite naturally reverted to that suit of Aztecan armour, and the glorious possibilities which the words of the exile had opened up to them as explorers.

Bruno listened with unfeigned interest, but not so his more mercurial brother, who took advantage of an opening left by the professor, to bluntly interject:

"What mighty good, even if you should find it all, uncle

Phaeton? You couldn't pick it up and tote it away, to start a dime museum with. And, as for my part, - I'll tell you what! If we could only find something like Aladdin's cave, now!"

"Growing miserly in your old age, are you, lad?" mocked his uncle.

"No; I don't mean just that. His trees were hung with riches, but mine should be - crammed and crowded full of plum pudding, fruit cake, angel food, mince pies, and the like! Yes, and there should be fountains of lemonade! And mountains of ice-cream! And sandbars of caramels, and chocolate drops, and trilbies, and - well, now, what's the matter with you fellows, anyway?"

He spoke with boyish indignation at that laughing outbreak, but the kindly professor quickly managed to smooth the matter over, although not before Waldo had promised Bruno a sound thumping the first time they set foot upon land.

Until past the noon hour that pleasant voyage lasted, without any remarkable discovery being made, the trio munching a cold lunch at their ease, rather than take the trouble to effect a landing.

But then, not very long after the sun had begun his downward course, there came a change which caused Featherwit's blood to leap through his veins far more rapidly than usual, for yonder, still a number of miles away, there was gradually opening to view a hill-surrounded valley of considerable dimension, certain portions of which betrayed signs of cultivation, or at least of vegetation different from aught the explorers had as yet come across since entering that land of wonders.

Almost unwittingly Professor Featherwit sent the air-ship higher, even as it sped onward at quickened pace, his face as pale as his eyes were glittering, intense anticipation holding him spellbound for the time being. And then - the

JOSEPH E. BADGER, JR.

wondrous truth!

"Behold!" he cried, shrilly, pointing as he spoke.

"Houses yonder! Cultivated fields, and - see! human beings in motion, who are -"

"Kicking up a great old bobbery, just as though they'd sighted us, and wanted to know - I say, uncle Phaeton, how would it feel to get punched full of holes by a parcel of bow-arrows?"

With a quick motion the air-ship was turned, darting lower and off at a sharp angle to its former course, for the professor likewise saw what had attracted the notice of his younger nephew.

Scattered here and there throughout that secluded valley were human beings, nearly all of whom had sprung into sudden motion, doubtless amazed or frightened by the appearance of that oddly shaped air-demon.

Brief though that view had been, it was sufficiently long to show the professor houses of solid and substantial shape, cultivated plots, human beings, and a little river whose clear waters sparkled and flashed in the sunlight.

It was very hard to cut that view so short, but the professor had not lost all prudence, and he knew that danger to both vessel and passengers might follow a nearer intrusion upon the privacy of yonder armed people. Yet his face was fairly glowing with glad exultation as he brought the aerostat to a lower strata of air, shutting off all view from yonder valley, as it lay amid its encircling hills.

"Hurrah!" he cried, snatching off his cap and waving it enthusiastically, as the air-ship floated onward at ease. "At last! Found - we've discovered it at last! And all is true, - all is true!"

"Found what, uncle Phaeton?" asked Waldo, a bit doubtfully.

"The Lost City of the Aztecs, of course! Oh, glad day, glad day!"

"Unless - what if it should prove to be only a - a mirage, uncle Phaeton?" almost timidly ventured Bruno, a moment later.

CHAPTER XV.

ASTOUNDING, YET TRUE.

The professor gave a great start at this almost reluctant suggestion, shrinking back with a look which fell not far short of being horrified. But then he rallied, forcing a laugh before speaking.

"No, no, Bruno. All conditions are lacking to form the mirage of the desert. And, too; everything was so distinct and clearly outlined that one could -"

"Fairly feel those blessed bow-arrows tickling a fellow in the short ribs," vigorously declared the younger Gillespie. "Not but that - I say, uncle Phaeton?"

"What is it now, Waldo?"

"Reckon they're like any other people? Got boys and - and girls among 'em, I wonder?"

"I daresay, yes, why not?" answered Featherwit, scarcely realising what words were being shaped by his lips, while Bruno broke into a brief-lived laugh, more at that half-sheepish expression than at the query itself.

"Both boys and girls galore, I expect, Kid; but you needn't borrow trouble on either score. You can outrun the lads, while as for the fairer sex, - well, they'll take precious good care to keep well beyond your reach, - especially if you wear such another fascinating grin as -"

"Oh, you go to thunder, Bruno Gillespie!"

Through all this interchange the air-ship was maintaining a wide sweep, drawing nearer the forest beneath, if only to keep hidden from the eyes of the strange people in yonder deep valley. Yet the gaze of Phaeton Featherwit as a rule kept turned towards that particular point, his eyes on fire, his lips twitching, his whole demeanour that of one who feels a discovery of tremendous importance lies just before him.

"Are we going to land, uncle Phaeton?" queried Bruno, taking note of that preoccupation, which might easily prove dangerous under existing circumstances.

That question served to recall the professor to more material points, and, after a keen, sweeping look around, he nodded assent.

"Yes, as soon as I can discover or secure a fair chance. I wish to see more - I must secure a fairer view of the - of yonder place."

"Will it not be too dangerous, though? Not for us, especially, uncle, but for the aerostat? Even if these be not the people you imagine -"

"They are past all doubt a remnant of the ancient Aztecs. Yonder lies the true Lost City, and we are - oh, try to comprehend all that statement means, my lads! Picture to yourselves what boundless fame and unlimited credit awaits our report to the outer world! The benighted world! The besotted world! The - the -"

"While we'll form the upsotted world, or a portion of it, without something is done, - and that in a howling hurry, too!" fairly spluttered Waldo, as the again neglected air-ship sped swiftly towards a more elevated portion of that earth, part of the tall hill-crest which acted as nature's barricade to yonder by nature depressed valley.

"Time enough, lad, time enough, since we are going to land," coolly assured the professor, deftly manipulating the steering-gear and still curying around those tree-crowned hills. "If we are really hunted after, 'twill naturally be in the quarter of our vanishment, while by alighting around yonder, nearly at right angles with our initial approach, we will have naught to fear from the - the Aztecan clans!"

Clearly the professor had settled in his own mind just what lay before them, and nothing short of the Lost City of the Aztecs would come anywhere near satisfying that exalted ideal. And, taking all points into full consideration, was there anything so very absurd in his method of reasoning, or of drawing a deduction?

Still, that exaltation did not prevent uncle Phaeton from taking all essential precautions, and it was only when an especially secure landing-place was sighted that he really attempted to touch the earth.

Fully one-half of that wide circuit had been made, and as nothing could be detected to give birth to fears for either self or air-ship, the aeronauts skilfully landed their vessel with only the slightest of jars. It was a well-screened location, where naught could be seen of the flying-machine until close at hand, yet so arranged as to make a hasty flight a very easy matter should the occasion ever arise.

Not until the landing was effected and all made secure, did Professor Featherwit speak again. Then it was with gravely earnest speech which suitably affected his nephews.

"Above all things, my dear lads, bear ever in mind this one fact, - we are not here to fight. We do not come as conquerors, weapons in hand, hearts filled with lust of blood. To the contrary, we are on a peaceful mission, hoping to learn, trusting to enlighten, with malice towards none, but honest love for all those who may wear the human shape, be they of our own colour or - or - otherwise."

"That's what's the matter with Hannah's cat!" cheerfully chipped in the irrepressible Waldo. "I say, uncle Phaeton, is it just a lie-low here until yonder fellows grow tired of looking for what they can't find, then a flight on our part; or will we - "

"Have we voyaged so far and seen so much, to rest content with so very little?" exclaimed the professor, hardly as precise of speech as under ordinary conditions. "No, no, my lads! Yonder lies the greatest discovery of the nineteenth century, and we are - Get a hustle on, boys! The day is waning, and with so much to see, to study, to - Come, I say!"

In spite of his initial attempt to impress his nephews with a due sense of the heavy responsibilities which rested upon them, Phaeton Featherwit was far more excited than either one of the brothers. Doubtless he more nearly appreciated the importance of this wondrous discovery, provided his now firm belief was correct, - that yonder stood a solid, substantial city, erected by the hands of a people whom common consent had agreed were long since wiped out of existence.

The story told by Cooper Edgecombe, backed up by the articles taken from the person of the warrior whom he had slain in self-defence, certainly had its weight; while the brief and imperfect glimpse which he had won of yonder valley helped to bear out that astounding belief. And yet, how could it be true?

Really believing, yet forced by more sober reason to doubt, the poor professor was literally "in a sweat" long ere another view could be won of the depressed valley, although the landing of the air-ship was so well chosen as to make that trip of the briefest duration consistent with prudence.

JOSEPH E. BADGER, JR.

The natural obstacles were considerable, however, and as they picked their way along, the brothers for the first time began to gain a fairly accurate idea of what was meant by the term, a virgin forest.

To all seeming, the human foot had never ventured here, nor were any marks or spoor of wild beasts perceptible on either side.

Although the aerostat had landed not far below the crest of those hills, the adventurers had to climb higher, before winning the coveted view, partly because the most practicable route led down into and along a winding gulch, where the footing was far less treacherous than upon the higher ground, cumbered, as that was, with the leaf-mould of centuries.

Still, half an hour's steady labour brought the little squad to the coveted point, and once again Professor Featherwit was almost literally stricken speechless, - for there, far below their present location, spread out in level expanse, lay the secret valley with all its marvels.

Far more extensive than it had appeared by that initial glimpse, the valley itself seemed composed of fertile soil, yet, by aid of the river which cut through, near its centre, irrigating ditches conveyed water to every acre, thus ensuring bounteous crops of grain and of fruit as well.

Numerous buildings stood in irregular array, for the most part of no great height, nor with many pretensions towards architectural beauty or grace of outline; but in the centre of the valley upreared its head a massive structure, pyramidal in shape, consisting of five comparatively narrow terraces, connected one with another only at each of the four corners, where stood a wide-stepped flight of stones.

"Behold!" huskily gasped the professor, intensely excited, yet still able to control the field-glass through which he was eagerly scanning yonder marvels. "The temple of the gods! And, yonder, the temple of sacrifice, unless my memory is - and look! The people are - they wear just such garb as - Oh, marvellous! Amazing! Astounding! Incredible - yet true!"

Although their uncle could thus take in the various details to better advantage, still the intervening distance was not so great as to entirely debar the brothers from finding no little to interest them, as was readily proven by their various exclamations.

"Just look at the people, will ye, now? Flopping around like they hadn't any bigger business than to - Reckon they're looking for us to come back, Bruno?"

"Or watching for the monster bird of prey, rather," suggested the elder Gillespie. "Of course they couldn't distinguish our faces, and our bodies were fairly well hidden. And, even more, of course, they must be totally ignorant of all such things as flying-machines and the like."

"Poor, ignorant devils!" sympathetically sighed the youngster. "Well, we'll have to do a little missionary work in this quarter, before taking our departure, eh, uncle Phaeton?"

With a start, Featherwit descended out of the clouds in which he had been lost ever since winning a fair view of the secret city; and now, rallying his wits and fairly aglow with eager interest in this marvellous discovery, he began pointing out the various objects of special importance, naming them with glib assurance, then reminding the boys how wonderfully similar all was to what had existed in Old Mexico before the conquest.

Bruno listened with greater interest than his brother could summon at will. For one thing, he had long been a lover of the genial Prescott, and, now that his memory was freshened in part, was able to closely follow the course of that little lecture, noting each strong point made by the professor in bolstering up his delightful theory.

That monologue, however, was abruptly broken in upon by Waldo, who gave an eager exclamation, as he reached forth a pointing finger:

"Look! There's a white woman yonder, - two of 'em, in fact!"

CHAPTER XVI.

CAN IT BE TRUE?

That announcement came with all the force of a bolt from the blue, and even the professor dropped his glasses with a gasp of amazement, while Bruno would have leaped to his feet, only for the hasty grab which his brother made at the tail of his coat.

"White - where? Surely it cannot be that - Edgecombe -"

"Augh, take a tumble, boy!" ejaculated Waldo, giving a jerk that rendered compliance nearly literal, though scarcely full of grace. "Want to have the whole gang make a howling break this way? Want to - They're white all right, though!"

"Where? Which direction? Point them out, and - I fail to see anything which would bear out your -"

The professor was sweeping yonder field with his glass, searching for the primal cause of that latest excitement, but without success. No sign of a white face, male or female, rewarded his efforts, and he turned an inquiring gaze upon the youngster.

Waldo was peering from beneath the shade of his hand, but now drew back with a long breath, to slowly shake his head.

"They've gone now, but I did see them, and they were white,

JOSEPH E. BADGER, JR.

just as white as - as anything!"

Bruno frowned a bit at that unsatisfactory conclusion, but the professor was of more equable temper, for a wonder. He smilingly shook his head, while gazing kindly, then spoke:

"I myself might have made the same error, Waldo, but you surely were in error, for once."

"What! You mean I never saw those white women, uncle Phaeton?"

"No, no, I am not so seriously faulting your eyesight, my dear boy," came the swift assurance. "But even the best of us are open to errors, and there were in olden times not a few Aztecs with fair skins; not exactly white, yet comparatively fair when their race was considered. And, no doubt, Waldo, you saw just such another a bit ago."

But the youngster was not so easily shaken in his own opinion.

"There were a couple of 'em, not just such another, uncle. And they were white, - pure white as ever the Lord made a woman! And - why, didn't I see their hair, long and floating loose? And wasn't that yellow as - as gold, or the sunshine itself?"

"Yellow hair?"

"Yes, indeedy! Yellow hair, white skins, - faces, anyway. Blondes, the couple of 'em; and to that I'll make my davy!"

And so the youngster maintained with even more than usual sturdiness, when questioned more closely, pointing out the very spot upon which the strange beings were standing, the top of a large, tall building, clearly one of the series of temples.

In vain the field-glass was fixed upon that particular point. The partly roofed azotea was wholly devoid of human life, and though watch was maintained in that direction for many minutes thereafter, by one or other of the air-voyagers, naught was seen to confirm the assertion made by the younger Gillespie.

For the moment that fact or fancy dominated all other interests, for, granting that Waldo had not been misled by a naturally fair Indian face, there was room for a truly startling inference.

"Could it actually be they?" muttered Bruno, face pale and eyes glittering with intense interest. "Could they have escaped with life from the balloon, and been here ever since?"

"You mean -"

"The wife and child of Cooper Edgecombe, - yes! Who else could they be, unless - I'd give a pretty penny for one fair squint at them, right now! If there was only some method of - It would hardly do to venture down yonder, uncle Phaeton?"

The professor gave a stern gesture of denial, frowning as though he anticipated an actual break for yonder town, in spite of the odds against them.

"That would be madness, Bruno! Worse than madness, by far! Look at yonder warriors, all thoroughly armed, and eager to drink blood as ever they were in centuries gone by! They are hundreds, if not thousands, while we are but three! Madness, my boy!"

"Four, with Mr. Edgecombe, uncle."

"And that means a complete host so long as we are backed up by the air-ship," declared Waldo, in his turn. "Those fellows!" with a sniff of true boyish scorn for aught that was not fully up to date. "What could they do, if we were to open fire on them just once?"

"Prove our equals, man for man, armed as they assuredly are," just as vigorously affirmed the professor, inclined rather to magnify than diminish the importance of these, his so recently discovered people. "You forget how the Aztecans fought Cortez and his mailed hosts. Yet these are one and identical, so far as valour and training and blood can go."

"Huh! Scared of a runty horse so badly that they prayed to 'em as they did to their own gods!" sniffed Waldo, betraying a lore for which he did not ordinarily receive fair credit. "Why, uncle Phaeton, let you just slam one o' those dynamite shells inside a chief -"

"Nay, Waldo, must I repeat, we are not here for the purpose of conquest, unless by purely amicable methods. There must be no fighting, for or against. Savages though most people would be inclined to pronounce yonder race, they are human, with souls and -"

"But I always thought they were heathens, uncle Phaeton?"

The professor subsided at that, giving over as worse than useless the attempt to enlighten the irrepressible youngster, at least for the time being.

Silence ruled for some little time, during which each one of the trio kept keen watch over the valley, the field-glass changing hands at intervals in order to put all upon an equal footing.

One thing was clear enough unto all: the Indians had been greatly wrought up by the brief appearance of some queerly shaped monster of the air, and while a goodly number of their best warriors had hastened out of the valley and up the difficult passes, in hopes of learning more, still others were astir, weapons in hand, evidently determined to defend their lives or their property from any assault, should such be made, whether by known or foreign adversaries.

This busy stir and bustle, combined with the novel architecture and so many varying points of interest, would have been a mental and visual feast for the trio of air-voyagers, only for that one doubt: were white captives actually in yonder temple? And, if white, were they the long-lost relatives of the aeronaut, Cooper Edgecombe?

Quite naturally the interest displayed by the Indians centred in the quarter of the heavens where that air-demon had been sighted, hence our friends saw very little cause for apprehension on their own parts.

Thus they were given a better opportunity for thinking of and then discussing the new marvel.

Again did Waldo vow that his eyes had not befooled him. Again he positively asserted that he had seen two white women, wearing blonde hair in loose waves far adown their backs. And once again Bruno, in half-awed tones, wondered whether or no they were the mother and child borne away upon the wings of a mighty storm, fifteen long years gone by.

"It is possible, though scarcely credible," admitted uncle Phaeton, in grave tones, as he wrinkled his brows after his peculiar fashion when ill at ease in his mind. "Edgecombe lived through just such another experience; though, to be sure, he was a man of iron constitution, while they were far more delicate, as a matter of course."

"Still, it may have happened so?" persisted Bruno, taking a strong interest in the matter. "You would not call it too far-fetched, uncle?"

"No. It may have happened. I would rather call it marvellous, yet still possible. And if so -"

"There is but a single answer to that supposition, uncle; they must be rescued from captivity!" forcibly declared Bruno.

"That's right," confirmed Waldo. "Of course all women and girls - I mean other people's kin - are a tremendous sight of

JOSEPH E. BADGER, JR.

bother and worry, and all that; but we're white, and so are they."

"We must rescue them; there's nothing else to do," again emphasised the elder Gillespie.

"That is no doubt the proper caper, speaking from your boyish point of view, my generous-hearted nephews; but - just how?" dryly queried the professor. "Have you arranged all that, as well, Bruno?"

"You surely would not abandon them, uncle Phaeton?" asked the young man, something abashed by that veiled reproof. "To such a horrible fate, too?"

"A fate which they must have endured for fifteen years, provided your theory is correct, Bruno," with a fleeting smile. "Don't mistake me, lads. I am ready and willing to do all that a man of my powers may, provided I see just and sufficient cause for taking decisive action. That is yet lacking. We are not certain that there are white women yonder. Or, if white women, that they are captives. Or, if captives, that they would thank us for aiding them to escape."

"Why, uncle Phaeton! Think of Mr. Edgecombe, and how -"

"I am thinking of him, and I wish to think yet a little longer," quietly spoke the professor. "keep a lookout, lads, and if you see aught of Waldo's fair women, pray notify me."

For the better part of an hour comparative silence reigned, the boys feasting eyes upon yonder spectacle, their uncle deeply in reverie; but then he roused up, his final decision arrived at.

"I will do it!" were his first words. "Yes, I will do it!"

"Do what, uncle Phaeton?" asked Waldo, with poorly suppressed eagerness, as he turned towards his relative.

"Go after Cooper Edgecombe, - bringing him here in order that he may, sooner or later, solve this perplexing enigma. Come, boys, we may as well start back towards the aerostat."

But both youngsters objected in a decided manner, Waldo saying:

"No, no, uncle Phaeton! Why should we go along? You'll be coming right back, and will be less crowded in the ship if we don't go."

"And we can better wait right here; don't you see, uncle?"

"To keep the Lost City safely found, don't you know? What if it should take a sudden notion to lose itself again?" added Waldo, innocently.

CHAPTER XVII.

AN ENIGMA FOR THE BROTHERS.

In place of the indulgent smile for which he was playing, Waldo received a frown, and directly thereafter the professor spoke in tones which could by no possibility be mistaken.

"Come with me, both of you. I am going back to the aerostat, and I dare not leave you boys behind. Come!"

Kind of heart and generally complaisant though uncle Phaeton was, neither Bruno nor Waldo cared to cross his will when made known in such tones, and without further remonstrance they followed his lead, slipping away from the snug little observatory without drawing attention to themselves from any of yonder busy horde.

Not until the trio was fairly within the gulch did the professor speak again, and then but a brief sentence or two.

"Give me time to weigh the matter, lads. Possibly I may agree, but don't try to hurry my cooler judgment, please."

Waldo gave his brother an eager nudge at this, gestures and grimaces being made to supply the lack of words. But when, the better to express his confidence that all was coming their way, the youngster attempted a caper of delight, his foot slipped from a leaf-hidden stone, and he took an awkward tumble at full length.

"Never touched me!" he cried, scrambling to his feet ere a hand could come to his aid. "Who says I don't know how to stand on both ends at the same time?"

Barring this little caper, naught took place on their way to the air-ship; and once there, the professor heaved a mighty sigh, wiping his heated face as one might who has just won a worthy race. But he betrayed no especial haste in setting the flying-machine afloat and Waldo finally ventured:

"Can we help you off, uncle Phaeton?"

But he was assured there existed no necessity for such great haste.

"In fact, it might be dangerous to start while so many of the Aztecs are upon the lookout," came the unexpected addition. "I believe it would be vastly better not to leave here until shortly before dawn, to-morrow."

It took but a few words further to convince the brothers that this idea was wisest, and while the young fellows felt sorry to have their view cut so short, neither ventured to actually rebel.

After all, the day was well-nigh spent, and, besides preparing their evening meal, it was essential that their plans for the immediate future should be shaped as thoroughly as possible.

Professor Featherwit had resolved to fetch Cooper Edgecombe to the scene of interest, in order to give him at least a fair chance to solve the enigma which was perplexing them all. Even so, he felt that no small degree of physical danger would attend that presence, particularly if it should really prove, as they could but suspect, that both wife and daughter of the involuntary exile were yonder, among the Aztecans.

Much of this the professor made known to his nephews during that evening, the trio thoroughly discussing the matter in all its bearings, but before the air-ship was prepared for the night's rest, uncle Phaeton made the youngsters happy by consenting to their remaining behind as guardians to the Lost City, while he went in quest of the balloonist.

"But bear ever in mind the conditions, lads," was his earnest conclusion. "I place you upon your honour to take all possible precautions against being discovered, or even running the least unnecessary risk during my absence."

"Don't let that bother you, uncle Phaeton," Waldo hastened to give assurance. "We'll be wise as pigeons, and cautious as any old snake you ever caught up a tree; eh, Bruno, old man?"

"We promise all you ask, uncle, but does that mean we must stay right here, without even stealing a weenty peep at the Lost City?"

Professor Featherwit felt sorely tempted to say yes, but then, knowing boyish nature (although Bruno had just passed his majority, while Waldo was "turned seventeen") so well, he feared to draw the reins too tightly lest they give way entirely.

"No; I do not expect quite that much, my lads; but I do count on your taking no unnecessary risks, and in case of discovery that you rather trust to flight, and my finding you later on, than to actually fighting."

So it was decided, and at a fairly early hour the trio lay down to sleep. Although so unusually excited by the marvellous discoveries of the day just spent, their open-air life tended to calm their brains, and, far sooner than might have been expected, sleep crept over them, one and all, lasting until nearly dawn.

Perhaps it was just as well that the wakening was not more early, for the professor was beginning to regret his weakness of the past evening, and had there been more time for drawing lugubrious pictures of probable mishaps, he might even yet have insisted on taking the youngsters with him.

Knowing that it was rather more than probable some of the Indians would be stationed upon the hills to watch for the queerly shaped air-demon, the professor felt obliged to lose no further time, and so the separation was effected, just as the eastern sky was beginning to show streaks and veins of a new day.

"Touch and go!" cried Waldo, with a vast inhalation as he watched the aeromotor sail away with the swiftness of a bird on wing. "And for a weenty bit I reckoned 'twas you and me as part of the go, too!"

In company the lads enjoyed a more leisurely meal than their relative had dared wait for, knowing that, at the very least, they would have the whole of that day to themselves, so far as uncle Phaeton was concerned. As a matter of course, he would not attempt to return except under cover of night, or in the early dawn of another day.

All that had been thoroughly discussed and provided for the evening before, and was barely touched upon by the brothers now. Their first and most natural thought was of yonder Lost City, with its inhabitants, red, white, and yellow, as Waldo put it; but being still under the foreboding fears of the professor, they finally agreed to remain where he left them until after the sun crossed its meridian.

It was a rather early meal which the brothers prepared, if the whole truth must be told; and the last fragments were bolted rather than chewed, feet keeping time with jaws, as they hastened towards the observatory.

There was pretty much the same sort of view as on the day before, the main difference being that many of the Indians were labouring in the fields, instead of watching for the air-demon.

Using the glass by turns, the lads kept eager watch for the white women whom Waldo stubbornly persisted were within the town; but hour after hour passed without the desired reward, and Bruno began to doubt whether there was any such vision to be won.

"The sun was in your eyes, and you let mad fancy run away with your better judgment, boy," he decided, at length. "If not, why - what now?"

For Waldo gave a low, eager exclamation, gripping the field-glass as though he would crush in the reinforced leather case. A few moments thus, then he laughed in almost fierce glee, thrusting the glass towards his brother, speaking excitedly:

"A crazy fool lunatic, am I? Well, now, you just take a squint at the old house for yourself and see if - biting you, now, is it?"

For Bruno showed even more intense interest as he caught the right line, there taking note of - yes, they surely were white women! Faces, hair, all went to proclaim that fact. And more than that, even.

"Fair - lovely as a painter's dream!" almost painfully breathed the elder Gillespie. "I never saw such a lovely -"

"Injun squaw, of course. Couple of 'em. Nobody but a fool would ever think different. The idea of finding white women -"

"They are ladies, Waldo! I never saw such - and I feel that they must be the ones lost by poor Edgecombe when that storm -"

"That's all right enough, old fellow," interrupted Waldo, claiming the glass once more. "No need of your playing the porker on legs, though, as I see. Give another fellow a chance to squint. But aren't they regular jo-dandies, though, for a fact?"

The two women in question, clad in flowing robes of white, lit up here and there by a dash of colour, were slowly pacing to and fro upon the temple where first discovered by the keen-eyed youngster. Thanks to the excellent glass, it was possible to view them clearly in spite of the distance, and there could be no dispute upon that one point: both mother and daughter (granting that such was their relationship) were more than ordinarily fair and comely of both face and person.

For the better part of an hour that slow promenade lasted, and until the women finally passed beyond their range of vision, the brothers took eager and copious notes. Then, in spite of the fact that scores of other figures still came within their field of vision, curiosity lagged.

"It's like watching a street medicine show, after hearing Patti or seeing Irving," muttered Bruno, drawing back and stretching his wearied limbs beyond possible discovery.

"Or the A B C class playing two-old-cat, after a league game of extra innings; right you are, my hearty!" coincided Waldo, feeling pretty much the same way, "only with a difference."

Shortly after this, Bruno suggested a retreat to the rendezvous, and for a wonder his brother agreed without amendment.

The brothers passed down to the gulch, which formed the easiest route to their refuge, saying very little, and that in lowered tones. The confirmation so recently won served to stir their hearts deeply, and neither boy could as yet see a way out of the labyrinth that discovery most assuredly opened up before them.

"Of course we can't leave them there to drag on such a wretched existence," declared Bruno. "We couldn't do that, even though we learned they held no relationship to Mr. Edgecombe. But - how?"

"I reckon it's - what?" abruptly spoke Waldo, gripping an arm and stopping short for a few seconds, but then impulsively springing onward again as wild sounds arose from no great distance.

A score of seconds later they caught sight of a huge grizzly bear in the act of falling upon a slender stripling, whose bronze hue as surely proclaimed one of the Aztec children from yonder Lost City.

What was to be done? Disobey their uncle, or leave this lad to perish?

CHAPTER XVIII.

SOMETHING LIKE A WHITE ELEPHANT.

Only a lad, slight-limbed and slenderly framed to the eye, yet for all that gifted with a gallant heart, else he surely must have been cowed to terror by the huge bulk of such a dire adversary at close quarters.

Instead of trying to find safety in headlong flight, the Indian stood at bay, with both hands firmly gripping the shaft of his copper-bladed spear, at far too close quarters for employing bow and arrows, while the copper knife in his sash was held in reserve for still closer work.

Snarling, growling, displaying its great teeth while clumsily waving enormous paws which bore talons of more than a finger-length, the bear was balanced upon its hindquarters, evidently just ready to lurch forward with striking paws and gnashing teeth.

Its enormous weight would prove more than sufficient to end the contest ere it fairly began, while a slight stroke from those taloned paws would both slay and mutilate.

No one was better aware of all this than the Indian lad himself, yet he took the initiative, swiftly darting his spear forward, lending to its keen point all the power of both arms and body. A suicidal act it certainly appeared, yet one which could scarcely make his position more perilous.

JOSEPH E. BADGER, JR.

An awful roar burst from bruin as he felt that thrust, the blade sinking deep and biting shrewdly; but then he plunged forward, striking savagely as he dropped.

The Indian strove to leap backward an instant after delivering his stroke, but still clung to the spear-shaft. This hampered his action to a certain degree, yet in all probability that stout ashen shaft preserved his life, which that wound would otherwise have forfeited.

The stroke but brushed a shoulder, nor did a claw take fair effect, yet the stripling was felled to earth as though smitten by a thunderbolt.

All this before the brothers could solve the enigma thus offered them so unexpectedly; but that fall, and the awful rage displayed by the wounded grizzly as he briefly reared erect to grind asunder the spearshaft, decided the white lads, and, temporarily forgetting how dangerously nigh were yonder Aztecan hosts, both Bruno and Waldo opened fire with their Winchester rifles, sending shot after shot in swift succession into the bulky brute, fairly beating him backward under their storm of lead.

Victory came right speedily, but its finale was thrilling, if not fatal, the huge beast toppling forward to drop heavily upon the young savage, just as he was recovering sufficiently from shock and surprise to begin a struggle for his footing.

Firing another couple of shots while rifle-muzzle almost touched an ear, the brothers quickly turned attention towards the fallen Indian, more than half believing him a corpse, crushed out of shape upon the underlying rocks by that enormous carcass.

Fortunately for all concerned, the young Aztec was lying in a natural depression between two firm rocks, and while his extrication proved to be a matter of both time and difficulty, saying nothing of main strength, success finally rewarded the efforts of our young Samaritans.

The grizzly was stone-dead. The Indian seemed but a trifle better, though that came through compression rather than any actual wounds from tooth or talon. And the brothers themselves were fairly dismayed.

Not until that rescue was finally accomplished did either lad give thought to what might follow; but now they drew back a bit, interchanging looks of puzzled doubt and worry.

"Right in it, up to our necks, old man! And we can't very well kill the critter, can we?"

"Of course not; but it may cause us sore trouble if -"

Just then the young Aztec rallied sufficiently to move, drawing a step nearer the brothers, right hand coming out in greeting, while left palm was pressed close above his heart. And - still greater marvel!

"Much obliged - me, you, brother!"

If yonder bleeding grizzly had risen erect and made just such a salutation as this, it could scarcely have caused greater surprise to either Bruno or Waldo, looking upon this being, as they quite naturally did, in the light of a genuine "heathen," hence incapable of speaking any known tongue, much less the glorious Americanese.

True, there was a certain odd accent, a curious dwelling upon each syllable, but the words themselves were distinctly pronounced and beyond misapprehension.

"Why, I took you for a howling Injun!" fairly exploded Waldo, then stepping forward to clasp the proffered member, giving it a regular "pump-handle shake" by way of emphasis. "And here you are, slinging the pure United States around just as though it didn't cost a cent, and you held a mortgage on the whole dictionary! Why, I can't - well, well, now!"

For once in a way the glib-tongued lad was at a loss just what to say and how to say it. For, after all, this surely was a redskin, and the professor had explicitly warned them against - oh, dear!

Was it all a dizzy dream? For the Aztec drew back, speaking rapidly in an unknown tongue, then sinking to earth like one overpowered by sudden physical weakness.

Bruno Gillespie, too, was recalling his uncle's earnest cautions, and now took prompt action. He quickly secured the weapons which had been scattered as the Indian fell before the grizzly's paw, then the brothers drew a little apart to consult together.

"What'll we do about it?" whisperingly demanded Waldo, keeping a wary eye upon yonder redskin. "You tell, for blamed if I know how!"

"We daren't let him go free, else he might fetch the whole tribe upon our track," said Bruno, in the same low tones, no whit less sorely perplexed as to their wisest course.

"No, and yet we can't very well kill him, either! If we hadn't come along just as we did, or if - but he's a man, after all! Who could stand by and see that ugly brute make a meal off even an Injun?"

Bruno cast an uneasy look around, at the same time deftly refilling the partly exhausted magazine of his Winchester.

"Load up, Waldo. Burning powder reaches mighty far, even here in the hills; and who knows, - the whole tribe may come helter-skelter this way, to see what has broken loose! And we can't fight 'em all!"

"Not unless we just have to," agreed the younger Gillespie, placing a few shells where they would be handiest in case of another emergency. "But what's the use of running, if we're to leave this fellow behind to blaze our trail? If he is our enemy -"

"No en'my; Ixtli friend, - heart-brother," eagerly vowed the young Aztec, once again startling the lads by his strange command of a foreign tongue.

He rose to his feet, though plainly suffering in some slight degree from that brief collision with the huge beast, and smiling frankly into first one face, then the other, took Bruno's hand, touched it with his lips, then bowed his head and placed the whiter palm upon his now uncovered crown.

In like manner he saluted Waldo, after which he drew back a bit, still smiling genially, to add, in slowly spoken words:

"You save Ixtli. Bear kill - no; you kill - yes! Ixtli glad. Sun Children great - big heart full of love. So - Ixtli never do hurt, never do wrong; die for white brother - so!"

More through gesticulation than by speech, the young Indian brave made his sentiments clearly understood, and if they could have placed full dependence in that pledge, the brothers would have felt vastly relieved in mind.

But they only too clearly recalled numerous instances of cunning ill-faith, and, in despite of all, they could not well avoid thinking that this was really something like a white elephant thrown upon their hands.

"All right. Play we swallow it all, but keep your best eye peeled, old man," guardedly whispered Waldo. "Fetch him along, yes or no, for it may be growing worse than dangerous right here, after so much shooting."

"You mean for us to -"

"Take the fellow along, and keep him with us, until uncle Phaeton comes back to finally decide upon his case," promptly explained Waldo. "Of course we ought to've let him die; ought, but didn't! We couldn't then, wouldn't now, if it was all to do over. So watch him so closely that he can't play tricks even if he wishes."

There was nothing better to propose, and though the job promised to be an awkward one to manage, Ixtli himself rendered it more easy.

Past all doubt he could understand, as well as speak, the English language, for he took a step in evident submission, speaking gently:

"Ixtli ready; heart-brother say where go, now."

Again the brothers felt startled by that quaintly correct accent, and almost involuntarily Bruno spoke in turn:

"You can talk English? When did you learn? And from whom?"

A still brighter smile irradiated the Aztec's face, and turning his eyes towards the secluded valley, he bowed his head as though in deep reverence, then softly, lovingly, almost adoringly, responded:

"SHE tell me how. Victo, - Glady, too. Ixtli know little, not much; his heart feel big for Sun Children, all time. So YOU, too, for kill bear, - like dat!"

Bruno turned a bit paler than usual, catching his breath sharply, as he repeated those names:

"Victo, - Glady, - Wasn't it by those names, Victoria, Gladys, that Mr. Edgecombe called his lost ones, Waldo?"

"I can't remember; but get a move on, old man. The sooner we're back where uncle Phaeton left us, where we can see a bit more of what may be coming, the safer my precious scalp will feel. This Injun -"

"No scalp," quickly interposed the Aztec, with a deprecatory gesture to match his words. "You save Ixtli. Ixtli say no hurt white brothers. Dat so, - dat sure for truth!"

Only partially satisfied by this earnest disclaimer of evil intentions, Waldo gripped an arm and hurried the Aztec along, leaving the bear where it had fallen, intent solely upon reaching a comparatively safe outlook ere worse could follow upon the heels of their latest adventure.

And Bruno brought up the rear as guard, eyes and rifle ready.

CHAPTER XIX.

THE CHILDREN OF THE SUN GOD.

No difficulty whatever was experienced in reaching that retreat, and milder prisoner never knew a guard than Ixtli proved himself to be, silently yielding to each impulse lent his arm by Waldo, smiling when, as sometimes happened, he was brought more nearly face to face with that armed rear-guard.

Nor were the Gillespie brothers worried by sound, sign, or token of more serious trouble from others of that strangely surviving race. And it was not long after reaching the rendezvous from which the professor had sailed in the early dawn, that the youngsters agreed the echoes of their Winchesters could not have reached the ears of the Lost City inhabitants.

"That's plenty good luck for one soup-bunch," quoth Waldo, yet adding a dubious shake of the head as he gazed upon their bronzed companion. "And if it wasn't for this gentleman in masquerade costume -"

"Ixtli friend. Ixtli feel like heart-brother," came in low, mellow accents from those smiling lips.

There certainly was naught of guile or of evil craft to be read in either eyes or visage, just then; but the brothers could not feel entirely at ease, even yet. How many times had warriors of his colour played a cunning part, only to end all by blow of tomahawk, thrust of knife, or bolt from the bended bow?

At a barely perceptible sign from Bruno, his brother drew apart, leaving their "white elephant" by himself, yet none the less under a vigilant guard.

"He seems all right, in his way," muttered the elder Gillespie, "but how far ought we to trust him, after what we promised uncle Phaeton?"

"Not quite as far as we can see him, anyway. Still, a fellow can't find the stomach to bowl him over like a hare, - without a weenty bit of excuse, at least."

"That's it! If he'd try to bolt, or would even jump on one of us, it would come far more easy. Look at him smile, now! And I hate to think of clapping such a bright-seeming lad in bonds!"

"Time enough for all that when he shows us cause," quickly decided Waldo, with a vigorous nod of his curly pow. "Pity if a couple of us can't keep him out of mischief without going that far. And we want to pump the kid dry before uncle Phaeton gets back; understand?"

Bruno gave a slight start at these words, but his eye-glow and face-flush bore witness that the idea thus suggested had not been unthought of in his own case.

"Then you really think -"

"That there's more ways than one of skinning a cat," oracularly observed Waldo. "Without showing it too mighty plainly, one or the other of us can always be ready and prepared to dump the laddy-buck, in case he tries to come any of his didoes. And, at the same time, we can be hugging up to him just as sweetly as though we knew he was on the dead level. Understand?"

Possibly the programme might have been a little more elegantly expressed, but Waldo, as a rule, cared more for substance than form, and his speech possessed one merit, that of perspicuity.

Having reached this fair understanding, the brothers dropped their aside, and moved nearer the young Aztec.

Ixtli gazed keenly into first one face, then the other, plainly enough endeavouring to read the truth as might be expressed therein, as related to himself. What he saw must have proved fairly satisfactory, since he gave another bright smile, then spoke in really musical tones:

"Good, - brother, now! That more good, too!"

In spite of the suspicions, which seem inborn where people of the red race are concerned, both Bruno and Waldo felt more and more drawn towards this remarkable specimen of a still more remarkable tribe; and not many more minutes had sped by ere the younger couple were chatting together in amicable fashion, although finding some little difficulty in Ixtli's rather limited vocabulary.

Not a little to his elder brother's impatience, Waldo apparently took a deeper interest in the recent adventure than in the subject which claimed his own busiest thoughts, but he hardly cared to crowd the youngster, lest he make matters even worse.

Aided by the sort of freemasonry which naturally exists between lads of an adventurous nature, Waldo readily succeeded in picking up considerable information from the Aztec, even before broaching that all-important matter.

Ixtli was the only son of a famed warrior and chieftain of the Aztecan clans, by name Aztotl, or the Red Heron. He, in common with so many of his people, had witnessed the approach and abrupt departure of the strange bird in the air, and had hastened forth in quest of the monster.

He failed to see aught more of the strange creature, but,

disliking to return home without something to show for the trip, remained out over night, then chanced to fairly stumble into the way of a mighty grizzly.

There were a few moments during which he might possibly have escaped through headlong flight, but he was too proud for that, and but for the timely arrival and prompt action on the part of his white brothers would almost certainly have paid the penalty with his life.

Then followed more thanks and broken expressions of gratitude, all of which Waldo magnanimously waved aside as wholly unnecessary.

"Don't work up a sweat for a little thing like that, old man. Of course we saw you were an Injun and - ahem! I mean, how in time did you happen to catch hold of our lingo so mighty pat, laddy-buck?"

"My brother means to ask who taught you to speak as we do, Ixtli?" amended Bruno, catching at the wished-for opportunity now it offered.

"And who was that nice little gal with the yellow hair? Is she - what did you call her? Gladys - And the rest of it Edgecombe?"

Waldo was eager enough now that the ice was fairly broken, but his very volubility served to complicate matters rather than to hasten the desired information.

Ixtli apparently thought in English pretty much as he spoke it, - slowly, and with care. When hurried, his brain and tongue naturally fell back upon his native language.

Sounds issued through his lips, but, despite all their animation, these proved to be but empty sounds to the eager brothers. And, divining the truth, Bruno checked his brother, himself acting as questioner, pretty soon striking the right chord, after which Ixtli fared very well.

Still, thanks to his difficulty in finding the right words with which to express his full meaning, it took both time and patience for even Bruno to learn all he desired; and even if such a course would be desirable, lack of space forbids giving a literal record of questions and answers, since the general result of that cross-examination may be put so much more compactly before the generous reader.

The first point made clear was that the young Aztec owed his imperfect knowledge of the English language to certain Children of the Sun, whom he named as if christened Victo and Glady. With this as starting-point, the rest formed a mere question of time and perseverance.

Growing in animation as he proceeded, Ixtli told of the coming to their city of those glorious children; riding upon the wings of an awful storm, yet issuing unharmed, unawed, bright of face, as the mighty orb the sons of Anahuac worshipped.

He told how an envious few held to the contrary: that these fair-skins had come as evil emissaries from the still more evil Mictlanteuctli, mighty Lord of Death-land, who had laden them with pestilence and brain-sorrow and eye-darkness, with orders to devastate this, the last fair city of the ancient race.

With low, sternly suppressed tones, the young warrior went on to tell of what followed: of the wicked attempt made by those malcontents to punish the bearers of death and misery; then, his voice rising and growing more clear, he told how, from a clearing-sky, there came a single shaft flung by the mighty hand of the great god, Quetzalcoatl, before which the impious dog went down in everlasting death.

"Struck by lightning, eh?" interpreted Waldo, who seemed born without the influence of poetry. "Served him mighty right, too!"

Bowing submissively, although it could be seen he scarcely comprehended just what those blunt words were meant to convey, Ixtli spoke on, seemingly with perfect willingness, so long as the adored "Sun Children" formed the subject-matter.

From his laboured statement, Bruno gathered that the sudden death of one who had dared to lift an armed hand against the woman so mysteriously placed there in their very midst awed all opposition to the general belief in the divine origin of mother and child; and ere long Victo was installed as a sort of high priestess of the temple more especially devoted to the Sun God.

That was long ago, and when Ixtli was but a child. As he grew older, and his father, Red Heron, was appointed as chief of guards to the Sun Children, Victo took more notice of the lad, and ended in teaching him both the English tongue and its Christian creed, so far as lay in his power to comprehend.

Then came less pleasing information concerning the Children of the Sun, which went far to prove that the death of one evil-minded dog had not entirely purged the Lost City, and it was with harsher tones and frowning brows that Ixtli spoke of the head priest, or paba, Tlacopa the evil-minded, who had built up a powerful and dangerous sentiment against both Victo and Glady, even going so far as to declare before the holy stone of sacrifice that the Mother of Gods demanded these falsely titled Children of the Sun.

"The fair-faced God must come soon, or too late!" sighed the Aztec, bowing his head in joined palms the better to conceal his evident grief. "He has promised to come, but hurry! They die - they die!"

This was hardly an acceptable stopping-point, but questioning was of little avail just then. Satisfied of so much, the brothers drew apart a short distance, yet keeping where they could guard their more or less dangerous charge, conversing in low tones over the information so far gleaned from the Aztec's talk.

"Well, we'll hold a tight grip on him, anyway, until uncle

Phaeton gets back," finally decided Waldo, speaking for his brother as well.

CHAPTER XX.

THE PROFESSOR AND THE AZTEC.

Fortunately for all concerned, there proved to be no serious difficulty attached to that same holding. So far as outward semblance went, Ixtli was very well content with both present quarters and present companionship.

He likewise enjoyed the supper that, aided by a small fire kindled in a depression so low that the light could by no means attract any unfriendly eye, Bruno prepared for them all. And just prior to taking his first taste, the young warrior bowed his head to murmur a few sentences which, past all doubt, had first come to his mind through the wonderful Victo: a simple little blessing, which certainly did not add to the dislike or uneasiness with which the brothers regarded their guest.

"He's white, even if he is red!" confidentially declared Waldo, at his first opportunity. "More danger of our spoiling him than his doing us dirt; and that's an honest fact for a quarter, old man!"

Bruno felt pretty much the same, yet his added years gave him greater discretion, and, in spite of that growing liking, he kept a fairly keen watch and ward over the Aztec.

After supper there came further questioning and answers, Waldo as a rule playing inquisitor, eager to learn more anent

JOSEPH E. BADGER, JR.

the strange existence which these people must live, so completely hemmed in from all the rest of the world as they surely were in yonder valley.

Without at all betraying the exile, Gillespie spoke of the lake and its mighty whirlpool, then learned that the Indians really made semi-annual trips thither for the purpose of laying in a supply of dried fish for the winter's consumption.

As the night waned, preparations were made for sleeping, although it was agreed between the brothers that one or the other should stand guard in regular order.

"Not that I really believe the fellow would play us dirt, even with every chance laid open," Waldo admitted. "Still, it's what uncle Phaeton would advise, and we can't well do less than follow his will, Bruno."

"Since we broke it so completely by tackling the grizzly," with a brief laugh.

"That's all right, too. Of course we'd ought to've skulked away like a couple of egg-sucking curs, but we didn't, and I'm mightily glad of it, too. For Ixtli - what a name that is to go to bed with every night, though! - for Ixtli is just about as white as they make 'em, nowadays; you hear me blow my bazoo?"

And so the long night wore its length along, the brothers taking turns at keeping watch and ward, but the Aztec slumbering peacefully through all, looking the least dangerous of all possible captives. And after this light even the cautious Bruno began to regard him ere the first stroke of coming dawn could be seen above the eastern hills.

Not being positive just where the air-ship would put in an appearance, since Professor Featherwit had, perforce, left that question open, to be decided by circumstances over which he might have no control, each guard in turn devoted considerable attention to the upper regions, hoping to glimpse the aerostat, and holding matches in readiness to raise a flare by way of alighting signal. But it was not until the early dawn that Bruno caught sight of the air-ship, just skimming the tree-tops, the better to escape observation by any Indian lookout.

After that the rest came easily enough. A couple of blazing matches held aloft proved sufficient cue to the professor, and soon thereafter the flying-machine was safely brought to land, so gently that the slumbers of the young Aztec were undisturbed.

Bruno gave a hasty word of warning and explanation combined, even before he extended a welcoming hand towards Mr. Edgecombe, who certainly appeared all the better for his encounter with people of his own race.

Professor Featherwit took a keen, eager look at the slumbering redskin, then drew silently back, to whisper in Bruno's ear:

"Guard well your tongue, lad. I have told him nothing, as yet, and we must consult together before breaking the news. For now we have had no rest, so I believe we would better lie down for an hour or two."

Mr. Edgecombe appeared to be perfectly willing to do this, and soon the wearied men were wrapped in blankets and sleeping peacefully.

Long before their lids unclosed, Bruno had an appetising meal in readiness, although the others had broken fast long before, and Ixtli, his hands tightly clasped behind his back, as a child is wont to resist temptation, was inspecting the air-ship in awed silence.

Taking advantage of this preoccupation, Bruno quickly yet clearly explained to his uncle all that had happened, showing that by playing a more prudent part the young warrior must inevitably have perished.

Then, making sure Cooper Edgecombe was not near enough to catch his words, Bruno told in brief the information gleaned from Ixtli concerning the Children of the Sun, whom he and Waldo more than suspected must be the long-lost wife and daughter of the exiled aeronaut.

As might have been expected, Professor Featherwit was deeply stirred by all this, fidgeting nervously while keeping alert ears, with difficulty smothering the ejaculations which fought for exit through his lips.

After satisfying his craving for food, the professor led the young Aztec apart from the rest of the party, speaking kindly and sympathetically until he had won a fair share of liking for his own, then broaching the subject of the Sun Children.

After this it was by no means a difficult matter to get at the seat of trouble, and little by little Featherwit satisfied himself that Ixtli would do all, dare all, for the sake of benefiting the woman and maiden who had treated him so kindly.

At a covert sign from the professor, Bruno came to join in the talk, and his sympathy made the young Aztec even more communicative. And Ixtli spoke more at length concerning Tlacopa, the paba, and another enemy whom the Children of the Sun had nearly equal cause to fear, one Huatzin, or Prince Hua, chiefest among the mighty warriors of the Aztecan clans.

This evil prince had for years past sought Victo for his bride, while his son, Iocetl, tried in vain to win the heart-smiles of the fair Glady, Victo's daughter. And, through revenge for having their suit frowned upon, these wicked knaves had joined hands with the priest in trying to drag the Sun Children down from their lofty pedestal.

It did not take long questioning, or shrewd, to convince the professor that in Ixtli they could count upon a true and daring supporter in case they should conclude to interfere in behalf of his patroness and teacher, adored Victo.

The professor led the way over to the air-ship, there producing the clothing and arms once worn by another Aztec warrior, which he had carefully stowed away in the locker, loath to lose sight of such valuable relics; truly unique, as he assured himself at the moment.

Bruno gave a little exclamation at sight of the articles, then in eager tones he made known the daring idea which then flashed across his busy brain.

"We ought to make sure before taking action, uncle Phaeton. Then why not let me don these clothes and steal down into the valley, under cover of darkness, to see the ladies and - "

"No, no, my lad," quickly interrupted the professor, gripping an arm as though fearful of an instant runaway. "That would be too risky; that would be almost suicidal! And - no use talking," with an obstinate shake of his head, as Bruno attempted to edge in an expostulation. "I will never give my consent; never!"

"Or hardly ever," supplied Waldo, coming that way like one who feels the proprieties have been more than sufficiently outraged. "Give some other person a chance to wag his chin a bit, can't ye, gentlemen? Not that *I* care to chatter merely for sake of hearing my own voice; but - eh?"

"We were considering whether or no 'twould be advisable to take a walk over to the observatory," coolly explained the professor. "Of course, if you would rather remain here to watch the aerostat -"

"Let Bruno do that, uncle. He grew thoroughly disgusted with what he saw over yonder, yesterday," placidly observed the youngster.

"Waldo, you villain!"

"Well, didn't you vow and declare that you could recognise

JOSEPH E. BADGER, JR.

grace and beauty and all other varieties of attractiveness only in - dark brunettes, old man?"

Professor Featherwit hastily interposed, lest words be let fall through which Mr. Edgecombe might catch a premature idea of the possible surprise held in store; and shortly afterwards the start was made for the snug covert from whence the Lost City had been viewed on prior occasions.

Naturally their route led them directly past the scene of the bear fight, where the huge carcass lay as yet undisturbed, and calling forth sundry words of wonder and even admiration, through its very ponderosity and now harmless ferocity.

Professor Featherwit deemed it his duty to gravely reprove his wards for their rash conduct, yet something in his twinkling eyes and in the kindly touch of his bony hand told a far different tale. His anger took the shape of pride and of heart-love.

In due course of time the lookout was won, and without delay the savant turned his field-glass upon the temple which appeared to appertain to the so-called Sun Children; but, not a little to his chagrin, the azotea was utterly devoid of human life.

But that disappointment was of brief existence, for, almost as though his action was the signal for which they had been waiting, mother and daughter came slowly into view, arm in arm, clad in robes of snowy white, with their luxuriant locks flowing loose as upon former occasions.

Both lads - three of them, to be more exact - gave low exclamations of eager interest as those shapes came in sight, while even Cooper Edgecombe gazed with growing interest upon the scene, wholly unsuspecting though he was as yet.

A slight nod from the professor warned the brothers to stand ready in case of need, then he offered the exile the glass, begging him to inspect yonder fair women upon the teocalli.

The glass was levelled and held firmly for a half minute, then the exile gave a choking cry, gasping, ere he fell as one smitten by death:

"Merciful heavens! My wife - my child!"

CHAPTER XXI.

DISCUSSING WAYS AND MEANS.

In good measure prepared for some such result, in case their expectations should prove true, friendly hands at once closed upon the exile, hurrying him back, and still more completely under cover, as quickly as might be.

Cooper Edgecombe seemed as wax in their hands, not utterly deprived of consciousness, but rather like one dazed by some totally unexpected blow. He made not the slightest resistance, yielding to each impulse given, shivering and weak as one just rallying from an almost mortal illness.

Yet there came an occasional flash to his eyes which warned the wary professor of impending trouble, and as quickly as might be the stunned aeronaut was removed from the point of observation, taken by short stages back to the spot where rested the flying-machine.

Ixtli seemed something awed by this (to him) inexplicable conduct on the part of the gaunt-limbed stranger, but gave his new-found friends neither trouble nor cause for worry, bearing them company and even lending a hand whenever he thought it might be needed.

The Gillespie brothers were far more deeply stirred, as was natural, but even Waldo contrived to keep a fair guard over his at times unruly member, speaking but little during that retreat.

With each minute that elapsed Cooper Edgecombe gained in bodily powers, and while his mental strength was slower to respond, that proved to be a blessing rather than otherwise.

The rendezvous was barely gained ere he gave a hoarse cry of reviving memory, then strove to break away from that friendly care, calling wildly for his wife, his daughter, fancying them in some dire peril from which alone his arms could preserve them.

It was a painful scene as well as a trying one, that which followed closely, and respite only came after bonds had been applied to the limbs of the madman, - for such Cooper Edgecombe assuredly was, just then.

There were tears in the professor's eyes, as he strove hardest to soothe the sufferer, assuring him that his loved ones should be restored to his arms, yet repeatedly reminding him that any rash action taken then must almost certainly work against their better interests.

The exile grew less violent, but that was more through physical exhaustion than aught else, and what had, from the very first, appeared a difficult enigma, now looked far worse.

Only when fairly well assured that the sufferer would not attract unwelcome attention their way through too boisterous shouting, did the professor draw far enough away for quiet consultation with his nephews.

Mr. Edgecombe was deposited within the air-ship, secured in such a manner that it would be well-nigh impossible for him to do either himself or the machine material injury, no matter how violent he might become; and hence, in case of threatened trouble from the inmates of the Lost City, flight would not be seriously hindered through caring for him.

Professor Featherwit now gleaned from his nephews pretty much all they could tell him concerning sights and events since his departure in quest of the exile. That proved to be very little more than he had already learned, and contained still less which seemed of especial benefit to that particular enigma awaiting solution.

True, Waldo suggested that Ixtli be employed as a medium of communication between the Sun Children and themselves; but, possibly because, as a rule, this irrepressible youngster's ideas were generally the wildest and most far-fetched imaginable, uncle Phaeton frowned upon the plan.

No; the young Aztec might prove true at heart, even as indications went, but the risk of so trusting him would prove far too great.

"That's just because you haven't known and slept with him, like we have," declared Waldo. "He's red on the outside, but he's got just as white a soul as the best of us, - bar none."

Bruno likewise appeared to think well of the young brave, and suggested an amendment to Waldo's motion, - that he accompany Ixtli into the sunken valley, covered by the friendly shades of night, there to open communication with the Sun Children.

"By so doing, we could make certain of their identity," the young man argued, earnestly. "That, it appears to me, is the first step to be taken. For, in spite of the apparent recognition by Mr. Edgecombe, it is possible that no actual relationship exists."

"What of that?" bluntly cut in the younger Gillespie. "Don't you reckon strangers'd like to take a little walk, just as well as any other people?"

"Patience, my lad," interposed the professor. "While we seem in duty bound to lend aid and assistance to women in actual distress, we can only serve them with their own free will and accord. Granting that the women we saw upon the teocalli were other than those believed by our afflicted friend -"

"But, uncle, look at their names! And don't Ixtli say - tell 'em all over again, pardner, won't ye?" urged Waldo, taking a burning interest in the matter, as was his custom when fairly involved.

The young Aztec complied as well as lay within his power, giving it as his fixed opinion that sore trouble, if not actual peril, awaited the Children of the Sun, unless assisted by powerful friends. He spoke of the mighty chieftain, Prince Hua, and of the high priest, Tlacopa, who was, to all seeming, playing directly into the hands of the 'Tzin.

"He say Mother of Gods call - loud! He say sacrifice, and dat - no, no! Quetzal' send - Quetzal' save - MUST save Victo, Glady!"

Further questioning resulted in but little more information, though, as Ixtli grew calmer, he emphasised such statements as he had already made, elaborating them a trifle. And, by this, his questioners learned that, humanly speaking, the fate of the Sun God's Children depended almost entirely upon the whim or fancy of the chief paba of the teocalli.

Through Tlacopa issued the awesome oracles, and when his voice thundered forth the dread fiat, who dared to openly rebel?

Further questioning brought forth one more important fact, - that there was absolutely no hope of either Victo or Glady coming forth from the valley, either by night or by day. While ostensibly free of will as they were of limb, neither woman was permitted to leave yonder temple, save under armed escort; and guards were on duty each hour of the day and night.

"But we could get to see and speak with them, Ixtli?" asked Bruno, eager to reach some fair understanding as to the future course of action.

"Yes, white brother, go with Ixtli," came the hesitating reply; but then the Aztec caught one of Gillespie's hands, holding it in close contrast to his own brown paw, shaking his head doubtingly.

"No like. Keen eye, dem people. Watch close. Find 'nother white skin - bad!"

"You hear that, Bruno?" asked the professor, really relieved at such positive evidence in conflict with the rash proposition made by the young man.

"Of course I thought of going under cover of the night, uncle, and surely it would not be such a difficult matter to darken my face and hands? With dirt, if nothing better can be found. And if I wore the clothes you brought from the cavern, uncle Phaeton?"

"That's the ticket!" broke in Waldo, eagerly. "Why, in a rig like that, I could turn the trick my own self!"

The consultation was broken off at this juncture by a faint summons from Cooper Edgecombe, and Professor Featherwit was only too glad of the excuse, hurrying over to the flying-machine, finding to his great joy that the exile was now far more like his old-time self.

Still, great caution was used in revealing all, and it was not until considerably later in the day that Mr. Edgecombe felt capable of taking part in the discussion of ways and means.

He declared that his recognition had been complete, in spite of the long years which had elapsed since losing sight of his dear ones; and he earnestly vowed to never give over until their rescue was effected, or he had lost his life while making the attempt.

While the two air-voyagers were thus engaged in talk, Bruno silently stole away with Ixtli, taking a bundle along, and leaving Waldo to throw their uncle off the track in case his suspicions should be prematurely awakened. Then, side by side, two Indian braves silently approached the aerostat, causing Professor Featherwit to make a hasty dive for his dynamite gun to repel a fancied onslaught.

"Sold again, and who comes next?" merrily exploded Waldo, dancing about in high glee as the supposed redskin slowly turned around for inspection before speaking, in familiar tones:

"Would there be such an enormous risk of discovery, uncle Phaeton, provided I put lock and seal upon my lips, save for the ladies?"

That experiment proved to be a complete success, and after Cooper Edgecombe added his pathetic pleadings to the young man's own arguments, Professor Featherwit gradually gave way, though still with reluctance.

"I could never find forgiveness should harm come to your mother's son, boy," he huskily murmured, his arm stealing about Bruno's middle. "I'd far rather venture myself, and - why not, pray?" as Waldo burst into an involuntary laugh.

Then he turned upon Ixtli, a hand resting upon each shoulder while he gazed keenly into those lustrous dark orbs for a full minute in perfect silence. Then he spoke, slowly, gravely:

"Can we trust you, friend? Would you sell the boy to whose arm you owe your own life, unto his enemies? Would you lead him blindly to his death, Ixtli, son of Aztotl?"

A wondering gaze, then the Indian appeared to flush hotly. He shook off those far from steady hands, drawing his knife and with free fingers tearing open his dress above the heart. Thrusting the weapon into Bruno's hand, he spoke in clear, distinct accents:

"Strike hard, white brother! Open heart; see if all black!"

Eye to eye the two youths stood for a brief space in silence, then the weapon was let fall, and Bruno gripped the Indian's hand and shook it most cordially.

"Strike you, Ixtli? I'd just as soon smite my brother by birth!"

"And that's mighty right, too!" cried Waldo, impetuously.

"I really begin to believe that you are all in the right, while I alone am left in the wrong," frankly admitted the professor.

CHAPTER XXII.

A DARING UNDERTAKING.

Still, that point was of too vital importance to justify hasty decision, and the professor did not make his surrender complete until the shades of another night were beginning to gather over the land.

Meantime, partly for the purpose of keeping the youngsters employed and thus out of the way of less harmless things, the professor suggested that the huge grizzly be flayed. If the proposed scheme should really be undertaken, that mighty pelt, if uncomfortable to convey, would serve as a fair excuse for the young brave's as yet unexplained absence from the Lost City.

As a matter of course, Cooper Edgecombe felt intense anxiety through all, but he contrived to keep fair mastery over his emotions, readily admitting that he himself could do naught towards visiting the Lost City.

"I know that my loved ones are yonder. I would joyfully suffer ten thousand deaths by torture for the chance to speak one word to - to them. And yet I know any such attempt would prove fatal to us all. The mere sight of - I would go crazy with joy!"

There is no necessity for repeating the various arguments used, pro and con, before the final agreement was reached. Enough

JOSEPH E. BADGER, JR.

has already been put upon record, and the result must suffice: Professor Featherwit yielded the vital point, and, having once fairly expressed his fears and doubts, flung his whole heart into perfecting the disguise which was now counted upon to carry Bruno safely into and out of yonder city.

He was carefully trigged out in the warlike uniform secured by Cooper Edgecombe at the cost of a human life, and, with fresh stain applied to his face and hands, the slight moustache he wore was not dangerously perceptible.

" 'Twould take a strong light and mighty keen eyes to see it at all, and even if a body should happen to notice it, he'd reckon 'twas a bit of smut, or the like," generously declared Waldo.

Under less trying circumstances, Bruno might have answered in kind, but now he merely smiled at the jester, then turned again to receive the earnest cautions let fall for his benefit by the professor.

Above all else, he was to steer clear of fighting, and, without he saw a fair chance of winning speech with the white women, he was to keep in such hiding as Ixtli might furnish, trusting the young Aztec to post the Children of the Sun as to what was in the wind.

Tremulous, almost incapable of coherent speech, so intense was his agitation, Cooper Edgecombe sent many messages to his loved ones, begging for one word in return. And if nothing less would serve -

His voice choked, and only his feverishly burning eyes could say the rest.

It was well past sunset ere the youngsters set forth from the rendezvous, accompanied a short distance by both Waldo and the professor; but the parting came in good time. It would be worse than folly to add to the existent perils that of possible discovery by some prowling Aztec who might work serious injury to them one and all.

That great bear-hide proved a tax upon their strength, even though the bullet-riddled head-piece had been carefully cut off and buried, lest those queer holes tell a risky tale on close examination; but Ixtli, as well as Bruno, was upborne by an exaltation such as neither had known before this hour.

There was nothing worse than the natural obstacles in the way to be overcome, and, knowing every square yard of ground so thoroughly, Ixtli chose the most practicable route to that hill-encircled town.

The stony pass was followed to the lower level, and the young adventurers had drawn fairly near the first buildings ere encountering a living being; and then ample time was given them for meeting the danger.

A low-voiced call sounded upon the night air, and Ixtli responded in much the same tone. Bruno, of course, was utterly in the dark as to what was being said, but he still held perfect faith in his copper-hued guide, and left all to the son of Aztotl.

The Aztec brave appeared to be explaining his unusually protracted absence, for he proudly displayed the great grizzly pelt, then exhibited the spear-head from which protruded the tooth-marked wood.

Like one who was already familiar with the details, Bruno slowly lounged forward a pace or two, then in silence awaited the pleasure of his companion on that night jaunt.

Ixtli was not many minutes in shaking off the Indian, and, almost staggering beneath his shaggy burden, moved away as though in haste to rejoin his family circle.

Fortunately for the venture, the Aztecans appeared to believe in the maxim of going to bed early, for there were very few individuals astir at that hour, young though the evening still was. And by the clear moonlight which fell athwart the valley, it was no difficult task to catch sight before being seen, where eyes so busy as those of the two young men were concerned.

Only once were they forced to make a brief detour in order to escape meeting another redskin, and then a guarded whisper from the lips of the Aztec warned Bruno that they were almost at the teocalli wherein the Children of the Sun made their home and abiding-place.

Leaving the grizzly pelt at a corner, for the time being, Ixtli led his white friend up and into the Temple of the Sun, pressing a hand by way of added caution.

Although he had declared that an armed guard was kept night and day over the Sun Children, and that he hoped to pass Bruno as well as himself without any serious difficulty, since he had long been a favoured visitor, and ever welcomed by Victo and Glady, the temple was seemingly without such protection upon the present occasion.

Ixtli expressed great surprise when this fact became evident, and he showed uneasiness as to the welfare of his beloved patroness and kindly teacher.

Surely something evil was impending! His father, Aztotl, was chieftain of the guards, and wholly devoted to the Sun Children, ready at all times to risk life in their behalf. Now, if the usual guards were lacking, surely it portended evil, - treachery, no doubt, at the bottom of which the paba and the 'Tzin almost certainly lurked.

All this Ixtli contrived to convey to Bruno, who fairly well shared that anxiety, but who was more for going ahead with a bold rush, to learn the worst as quickly as might be.

Still, unfamiliar with the construction of the temple as he was, Bruno felt helpless without his guide, and so timed his progress by that of Ixtli, right hand tightly gripping the handle of his "hand-wood," or maquahuitl, resolved to give a good account of either of those rascally varlets in case trouble lay ahead.

The unwonted desolation which appeared to reign on all sides was plainly troubling the Aztec brave, and he seemed to suspect a cunning ambuscade, judging from his slow advance, pausing at nearly every step to bend ear in keen listening.

Still, nothing was actually seen or heard until after the young men reached the upper elevation, upon a portion of which the Sun Children had been first sighted by the air-voyagers.

Here the first sound of human voices was heard, and Bruno stopped short in obedience to the almost fierce grip which Ixtli closed upon his nearest arm, listening for a brief space, then breathing, lowly:

"We see, first. Dat good! Him see first, dat bad! Eye, ear, two both. You know, brother?"

"You mean that we are to listen and play spy, first, Ixtli?" asked Bruno, scarcely catching the real meaning of those hurried words.

"Yes. Dat best. Come; step like snow falls, brother."

"Who is it, first?"

"Victo, she one. Odder man, not know sure, but think Huatzin. He bad; all bad! Kill him, some day. Dat good; plenty good all over!"

This grim vow appeared to do the Aztec good from a mental point of view, and then he led his white friend silently towards the covered part of the teocalli, from whence those sounds emanated.

Curtains of thick stuff served to shut in the light and to partly

JOSEPH E. BADGER, JR.

smother the sound of voices, but Ixtli cautiously formed a couple of peepholes of which they quickly made good use.

A portion of the sacred fire was burning upon its special altar, while a large lamp, formed of baked clay, was suspended from the roof, shedding a fair light around, as well as perfuming the enclosure quite agreeably.

Almost directly beneath this hanging-lamp stood the two Children of the Sun, one tall, stately, almost queenly of stature, and now looking unusually impressive, as she seemed to act as shield for her daughter, slighter, more yielding, but ah, how lovely of face and comely of person!

Even then Bruno could not help realising those facts, although his ears were tingling sharply with the harsh accents falling from a far different pair of lips, those of a tall, muscular warrior whose form was gorgeously arrayed in featherwork and cunning weaving, rich-hued dyes having been called to aid the other arts as well.

If this was actually the Prince Hua, then he was a most brutal sample of Aztecan aristocracy, and at first sight Gillespie felt a fierce hatred for the harsh-toned chieftain.

As a matter of course, Bruno was unable to comprehend just what was being said, thanks to his complete ignorance of the language employed; but he felt morally certain that ugly threats were passing through those thin lips, and even so soon his hands began to itch and his blood to glow, both urging him to the rescue.

Swiftly fell the reply made by Victo, and her words must have stung the prince to the quick, since he uttered a savage cry, drawing back an arm as though to smite that proudly beautiful face with his hard-clenched fist.

That proved to be the cap-sheaf, for Bruno could stand no more. He dashed aside the heavy curtain as he leaped forward, giving a stern cry as he came, swinging the war club over his shoulder to strike with all vengeance at the startled and recoiling Aztecan.

Only the young man's unfamiliarity with the weapon preserved Prince Hua from certain death. As it was, he reeled, to fall in a nerveless heap upon the floor, while, with a startled cry, another Aztec broke away in flight.

CHAPTER XXIII.

A FLIGHT UNDERGROUND.

That sudden appearance and flight of another man took Ixtli even more by surprise than it did Bruno, for he never even suspected such a possibility, knowing Prince Hua so well. Still, the young brave was swift to rally, swift to pursue, sending a menace of certain death in case the fleeing cur should not yield himself.

Just then Bruno had eyes and thoughts for the Sun Children alone, who quite naturally shrunk back in mingled surprise and alarm at his unceremonious entrance. He forgot his disguise, forgot everything save that before him stood the fair beings whom he had vowed to save at all hazards from what appeared to him worse by far than actual death.

Gillespie never knew just what words crossed his lips during those first few seconds, but he saw that the women, in place of eagerly accepting his aid, were visibly shrinking, apparently more alarmed than delighted with the opportunity thus offered.

Doubtless this was caused mainly by that odd blending of Aztec and paleface, the colour and garb of the one joined to the tongue of the other; but the result might have been even worse, had not Ixtli hastened back to clear up more matters than one.

In spite of his utmost efforts, the second Indian had escaped with life, although he received a glancing wound from an arrow, as he plunged down towards the lower level; and nothing seemed more certain than that an alarm would right speedily spread throughout the town, if only for the purpose of hurrying succour to the Lord Hua.

All this rolled in swift words over Ixtli's lips, his warning finding completion before either of the women could fairly interrupt the young brave. But then the one whom Ixtli termed Victo spoke rapidly in his musical tongue, one strong white hand waving towards the now somewhat embarrassed Gillespie.

"He friend; come save you, like save Ixtli," the Aztec hurriedly made reply, with generous tact speaking so that Bruno could comprehend as well as the women. "He good; all good! Paba bad; 'Tzin more bad; be worse bad if stay here, Victo - Glady."

Thus given the proper cue, Bruno took fresh courage and, in as few words as might be, explained his mission. He spoke the name of Cooper Edgecombe, and for the first time that queenly woman showed signs of weakness, staggering back with a faint, choking gasp, one hand clasped spasmodically above her madly throbbing heart, the other rising to her temples as though in fear of coming insanity.

"He is well; he is safe and longing for his loved ones," Bruno swiftly added, producing the brief note which the exiled aeronaut had pressed into his hand at almost the last moment. "He wrote you that - here it is, and -"

"Make hurry, quick!" sharply interposed Ixtli, as ominous sounds began to arise without the Temple of the Sun God. "Dog git 'way, howl for more. Come here - kill like gods be glad."

With an evident effort Victo rallied, tones far from steady as she begged both young men to save themselves without thought of them.

"I thank you; heaven alone knows how overjoyed I am to hear from my dear husband, - my poor child's own father! And he is near, to - But go, go! Guide and protect him, Ixtli, for - Go, I implore you, sir!"

"But how - we haven't arranged how you are to be rescued, and I must understand -"

"Later, then; another time, through Ixtli," interrupted Mrs. Edgecombe, since there could no longer be a doubt as to her identity. "If found here 'twill be our ruin as well as your own. Go, and at once I fear that Lord Hua may -"

"He 'live yet," pronounced Ixtli, rising from a hasty examination o f the fallen chieftain. "Dat bad; much more worse bad! He dog; all over dog!"

"And I greatly fear he must have recognised you as one of a foreign race, in spite of your disguise," added the elder woman, trouble in her face even as it showed in her voice. "He will be wild for revenge, and I fear - Go, and directly, Ixtli!"

Bruno Gillespie was only too well assured that this latest fear had foundation on truth. Swiftly though he had wielded the awkward (to him) hand-wood, Huatzin had sufficient time to sight his assailant, and almost certainly had divined at least a portion of the truth.

Doubtless it would have been the more prudent course to repeat that blow with greater precision; but Bruno could not bring himself to do just that, even though the ugly cries were growing in volume on the ground level; and he felt that capture would be but the initial step to death, in all likelihood upon the great stone of sacrifice.

Imminent though their peril surely was, Bruno could not betake himself to flight without at least partially performing the duty for which he had volunteered; and so he took time to hurriedly utter:

"Watch from the top of the tower for the air-ship, and be ready to leave at any moment, I implore you - both!"

For even now his admiring gaze could with difficulty be torn away from yonder younger, even more lovely, visage; although as yet the maiden had spoken no word, even shrinking away from this strangely speaking Aztec as though in affright.

"Come, brother, or too late," urged Ixtli, almost sternly. "Save you, or Glass-eyes call Ixtli dog-liar. Come; must run, no fight; too big many for that."

And so it seemed, when the young men rushed away from the lighted interior and gained the uncovered space beyond. Loud cries came soaring through the night from different directions, and dim, phantom-like shapes could be glimpsed in hurrying confusion.

Apparently the majority only knew that trouble of some description was brewing, and that the centre of interest was either in or near the Temple of the Sun God; yet that was more than sufficient to place the white intruder in great peril, despite the elaborate disguise he wore.

Then with awful abruptness there came a sound which could only be likened to rolling thunder by one uninitiated, but which caused Ixtli to shrink and almost cower, ere gasping:

"The great war-drum! Now MUST go! Sacrifice if caught; come, white brother! See, dat more bad now!"

Those mighty throbs rolled and reverberated from the hills, filling the night air with waves of thunder, none the less awe-inspiring now that their true import was realised.

The entire population was aroused, and each building seemed

to cast forth an armed host, while, as through some magic touch, a circle of fires sprung up on all sides, beginning to illumine both valley and barrier.

Bruno stood like one appalled, really fascinated by this transformation scene for which he had been so poorly prepared; but Ixtli better comprehended their situation, and gripping an arm he muttered, hastily:

"Come, brother; stop more, make too late. Must hide, now. Dat stop go back way came. Come!"

Bruno roused himself with an effort, then yielded to the Aztec's guidance, crouching low as the brief bit of clear moonlight had to be traversed.

Instead of making for the steps which, as customary, reached from terrace to terrace at each corner, Ixtli crept to the centre, where the temple-side was cast into deepest shadow, then lowered himself by his arms, to drop silently to the broad path below.

A whispered word urged Bruno to imitate this action, and those friendly hands caught and steadied Gillespie as he took the drop. And so, one after another, the mighty steps were passed, both young men reaching the ground at the same instant, having succeeded in leaving the Temple of the Sun God without being glimpsed by an Indian of all those whom the sonorous drum-throbs had brought forth In arms.

"Whither now?" asked Bruno, in guarded tones, as he looked forth from shadow into moonlight, seeing scores upon scores of armed shapes flitting to and fro, all looking for the enemy, yet none able to precisely locate the trouble.

Just then a savage yell broke from the top of the temple, followed by a few fierce-sounding sentences, which Ixtli declared came from the Lord Hua, then adding:

"He say kill if catch, but dat - no! Come, white brother. Ixtli show how play fool dat dog; yes!"

"All right, my hearty. Is it a break for the hills? I reckon I can break through. If not - well, I'll leave some marks behind me, anyway!"

"No, no, dat bad! Can't go to hills; must hide," positively declared the young Aztec. "Come, now. Me show good place; all dead but we."

Evidently trusting to pass undetected where so many others were rushing back and forth in seeming confusion, Ixtli broke away from the shadow of the temple, closely followed by Gillespie, heading as directly as might be for the strange refuge which he now had in mind.

That proved to be a low, unpretending structure which was of no great extent, so far as Bruno's hasty look could ascertain. Still, that was not the time for doubting the wisdom of his guide, nor a moment in which to discuss either methods or means; and as Ixtli passed through a massive entrance, the paleface followed, giving a little shiver as the barrier swung to behind them.

"What sort of a place is it, anyway, Ixtli?" he demanded, but the Aztec was too hurried for words, just then, save enough to warn his companion in peril that they must descend deeper into the earth.

It was more of a scramble than a deliberate descent, for the gloom was complete, and Bruno had no time in which to feel for steps or stairs. Only for the aiding touch of his guide, he must have taken more than one awkward tumble ere that lower level was attained.

Then a breathing-spell was granted him, and, while Ixtli bent ear in listening to discover if pursuit was being made, Bruno drew a match from the liberal supply he had taken the precaution to fetch along, and, striking it, held aloft the tiny torch to view their present surroundings.

Only to give an involuntary start and cry as he caught indistinct glimpses of fleshless bones and grinning skulls, those grim relics of mortality showing upon every side as his wild eyes roved around.

Then a hand struck down the match, and a swift voice breathed:

"Dey come dis way. See us hide - come hunt, now, to kill!"

CHAPTER XXIV.

THE SUN CHILDREN'S PERIL.

Not until the two young men passed beneath those heavy curtains did either one of the Sun Children really give thought to their own possible peril, but stood close together, arm of mother about daughter as they listened to the ominous sounds without, so rapidly growing in force and number.

Then, just as the deep tones of the war-drum boomed forth upon the night air, the fallen Aztec betrayed signs of rallying wits, giving a low sound which might have been groan of pain or curse of baffled rage. Be that as it may, the sound served one purpose: Victoria Edgecombe (to append her correct name for the first time) drew her child farther away, her right hand reaching forth to pluck a light yet effective spear from where it lay against the wall.

"Mother, mother!" faintly panted the maiden, plainly at a loss to comprehend all that had so recently transpired. "What is it? What does it all mean? Surely that was Ixtli; and - the other?"

"A messenger from your father, child, and -"

"My father? I thought - he is not - not dead?"

"Thanks be to heaven, not dead!" with hysterical joy in face as in voice. "Alive, and seeking us, Gladys! Coming to rescue us from this death in life, and now - to your knees, my daughter;

to thy knees, and lift thanks unto the good Father who has at last listened to my moans!"

Again the war-drum boomed forth in an awesome roll, but all unheeding that ominous sound, paying no attention to the stirring of yonder savage, whose lacerated scalp was painting his face a deeper red than even nature intended, mother and daughter sank to their knees, lifting hands and hearts towards the All-Powerful, even as their gratitude floated towards the Throne of Grace.

Then arose the hoarse tones of Huatzin, bidding his allies find and slay without mercy; cursing the treacherous Aztec who had thus guided one of a strange tribe into the very heart of their beloved city.

With a short, fierce ejaculation, Victo sprang to her feet, right hand once again grasping shaft of javelin, its copper point gleaming ruddily in the rays of lamp as though already moistened by the heart-blood of yonder villain.

Far differently acted the maiden, her figure trembling with fear and wonder commingled, her lips slightly blanched as she clung closer to her mother. Yet through all ran a touch of girlish curiosity which helped shape the words now crossing her lips.

"Who was it, mother? Who could the stranger be? And whither has he gone?"

"With Ixtli, my child, and may the good God of our own people grant them both life and liberty! If I thought - your father, Gladys! Alive and looking for his beloved ones! See! from his own dear hand, and he says - Hold! who comes there?"

But the alarm appeared to be without actual foundation, for the sounds came no closer, remaining beyond the drapery past which Lord Hua had staggered only a few brief seconds before.

Gladys rallied more speedily than one might have expected, and she spoke with even greater interest than at first.

"My dear father, and alive? Oh, mother, why is he not here to - why should he send another? And that one - he spoke our dear language, mother; surely he is not - not as Ixtli?"

"No; he was of our own people, child, and I can hardly conceive how he came hither, save that Ixtli must have acted as guide."

"And those awful warriors!" shivering as the war-cries followed the muffled roar of the great drum. "If found, he will be slain!

Do you think there is any hope for him, mother? And he seemed so - so -"

"He is gone with Ixtli, and Ixtli is true to the very core," Victo hastened to give assurance. "I would rather trust him than many another of thrice his years and warlike experience. Ixtli is true; ay, as true and tried as his father, Aztotl!"

"Who loves you, mother, and would win -"

"Hush, child!" just a bit sharply interposed the elder woman, yet at the same time tightening that loving clasp. "Merely as the daughter of his Sun God, Quetzalcoatl, and - ha!"

Once again there came the echoes of rapid foot-falls beyond the heavy draperies, and again this Amazonian mother drew her superb form in front of her shrinking child, poising the javelin in readiness for stroke or casting, as might serve best.

A strong arm brushed the curtains aside sufficiently to admit its owner's passage, but the armed warrior stopped short at sighting the Sun Children, his proud head lowering, hands crossing over his broad bosom in token of adoration, - for it surely was more than mere submission to one held his superior.

With a low cry, Victo drew back a bit, weapon lowering as she recognised friend in place of enemy.

"It is you, Aztotl?" she spoke, in mellow tones. "I thought - did you remove the usual guards, this evening?"

"The blame falls to my share, Sun Child," the Red Heron made answer, with a meekness strange in one of his build and general appearance, that of a king among ordinary warriors.

"Not justly, nor through fault of your own, my good and true friend," the elder woman made haste to give assurance. "Not even thy lips shall speak slander of Aztotl the True-heart, my brother."

With a swift advance the Red Heron caught the unarmed hand, to bend over it until his lips barely brushed the soft, perfumed skin. Then he sank to one knee, bowing his head until his brow touched the floor beneath her sandalled feet.

Swiftly, gracefully, these movements were made, and where they would have appeared fulsome or degraded in some, with this warrior the effect was far from disagreeable to see or to experience.

Victo flushed warmly and drew back a little farther, for the memory of those words let fall by Gladys came back with unpleasant distinctness. And was she so certain that Aztotl looked upon her as merely a god-descended priestess?

The Red Heron arose easily, head rising proudly above his shapely shoulders as he met those great blue eyes, - eyes as pure and as fathomless as the cloudless sky in midsummer.

And then, more like one giving a bare statement of facts than one offering a defence for himself, Aztotl spoke of a faithless subordinate, who was guilty of either careless neglect, or worse.

"It may be that Tezcatl lost his wits through strong waters, Sun

Child, or even that he took evil pay from still more vile hands. You have seen the last of him, though, Child of Quetzal'l."

"You surely do not mean that -"

Aztotl lightly tapped the knife-hilt showing above his maxtlatl, coldly adding words to that significant gesture:

"There is no place for fool or traitor upon the body-guard of the Sun Children. Tezcatl sinned; he has paid full forfeit. And just so shall all others perish who dare cast an evil glance towards - ha!"

Another outcry arose from the other side of the curtained recess, and the Red Heron instantly sprang away in that direction, hands gripping weapons in readiness for instant use in case of need.

Almost as swiftly, Victo and the maiden followed, one through fear, the other through utter lack of fear, for herself.

Those savage cries came from the lips of none other than the chieftain whose now bare head bore significant traces of Bruno Gillespie's handiwork, and he seemed bent on rushing directly into the presence of the Sun Children, until Red Heron interposed, stern and icy-toned:

"Stand back, my Lord Hua!" he ordered, left hand advanced with open palm, but its dexter mate armed and ready for hot work if that must come. "Venture no closer, on thy peril, chief!"

Huatzin recoiled a bit, though that might have been more through surprise than because he feared this proud warrior. He gripped his knife-hilt, and partly drew the blade from its supporting sash. A hissing oath escaped his lips, and he crouched a trifle, as a wild beast gathers its deadliest force prior to making a death leap.

"Darest thou bar my path, Aztotl?" he cried, hoarsely. "Make way, I bid thee; make way, for I will see the Sun Children and -"

"Not so, my Lord Hua," coldly interrupted the master of guards, that warning palm still turned to the front. "You are here without law or leave, and know what the edict says: from the going to the return of the sun, these stones are sacred from all feet save those of the Sun Children and their regular bodyguard."

"What care I for laws? Or for such as thou, Red Heron? I will that such a thing shall be, and it comes to pass. And - thou dare to bar my way, Aztotl?"

"Ay. By words if they prove sufficient. By force if called for. By death if worst must come; even the death of a mighty chieftain like Lord Hua would not be too great a feat."

For a brief space it seemed as though Huatzin would make a leap to which there could be but one termination, death to one or to both. But Aztotl coldly spoke on:

"I have given you fair and friendly warning, Lord Hua. Go, now, while the path of peace lies open. Go, else I sound the call, and my guard will take you in charge, just as they would any other rascally intruder."

"Your precious son, for instance?" retorted the 'Tzin, viciously. "He came with one whom - one of a different race from our own, Aztotl! A traitor in thy own family, yet thou darest hint at -"

Aztotl lifted a bent finger to his lips, sounding a shrill, far-penetrating whistle. The response was prompt indeed, an armed force advancing with weapons held ready, awaiting only word from commander to punish that rash intruder by hurling him to death over the terraces.

Although nearly beside himself with fury, Huatzin glared defiance at both guard and its commander, then turned more directly upon the Sun Children, speaking in savage tones:

"Unto you, proud Victo, I'll either win you as my -"

"Go on, Lord Hua," coldly spoke the woman, as his voice choked.

"I'll win and wear you as my squaw, or else give you to the stone of sacrifice!" he snarled, then turned away as Aztotl motioned his guards to clear the temple of all intruders, then see that none other dared enter.

CHAPTER XXV.

WALDO GOES FISHING.

It was with stronger forebodings than he dared acknowledge even to himself, that Professor Featherwit watched the two young men out of sight in the early gloom, and scarcely had his nephew passed beyond hearing than uncle Phaeton would gladly have recalled Bruno.

Waldo made light of all fears, prophesying complete success, and even going so far as to predict Bruno's return accompanied by the Children of the Sun; enthusiastic words which set the exile to trembling with excess of joy and anticipation.

What, then, was the blank dismay of all when, floating through the night, came the hollow throbbing of yonder mighty war-drum, fetching each person to his feet and holding him spellbound for the first few seconds.

Cooper Edgecombe turned sick at heart, even while ignorant as to the method of sending forth that alarm, his hollow groan being the first sound to follow the simultaneous exclamation which burst from three pairs of lips as the surprise came. And but a breath later Waldo broke forth with the excited query:

"What is it? What's broken loose now? Surely - thunder?"

Only Professor Phaeton at once recognised the sound, through description, and each one of those swiftly succeeding strokes seemed falling upon his heart, bidding him mourn for his beloved nephew, upon whom his aged eyes had surely looked their last in this life!

Yet it was the professor who took prompt action, speaking sharply as he darted across to where the air-ship rested:

"Come; get aboard, and let us do what lies in our power. It was criminal to send the poor lad into the jaws of death, but now - hasten, there may be a chance, even yet!"

The call was still hot upon his lips when his two companions entered the aerostat, gripping tight the hand-rail as Professor Featherwit sent the vessel afloat with reckless haste. As by a miracle they escaped disaster through rushing into a bushy treetop, and that fact served to steady the aeronaut's nerves.

"On guard, uncle Phaeton!" cried Waldo, making a lucky snatch at his cap, which one of the stiff boughs brushed off his head.

"Ay, ay, lad," responded the man at the guiding-gear, as the air-ship shot onward and upward, now heading, as directly as was practicable, for the Lost City of the Aztecs. "That was the very lesson I needed. I am steady of nerve, now, and will show no lack, - heaven grant that we may not be for ever too late, though!"

"What do you reckon could have kicked up such a bobbery, uncle? And what - ugh!" as the wardrum's throbbings again swelled forth in grim alarm. "What in time is that, anyway?"

As briefly as might be, the professor explained, and almost for the first time Waldo felt a thrill of dread.

"If they've got Bruno, what will they do with him?"

That very dread was worrying uncle Phaeton, and already through his busy brain were flashing horrid pictures of

JOSEPH E. BADGER, JR.

punishment and sacrifice, of hideous scenes of torture, wherein the eldest son of his dead sister played a prominent role, perforce.

He dared not trust his tongue to make answer, just then, and sent the aeromotor onward at top speed, leaning far forward to win the earliest glimpse of - what?

He caught sight of blazing beacons fairly encircling the Lost City, forming a cordon through which no stranger could hope to pass unseen. He beheld hundreds of armed shapes rushing to and fro, plainly looking for some intruder or other enemy, yet almost as certainly failing as yet to make the longed-for discovery.

Not until that moment had uncle Phaeton dared indulge in even the shadow of a hope. The awful alarm seemed proof conclusive that poor Bruno had been taken, through the treachery of Ixtli.

Naturally enough, that was his first belief, but now, as the air-ship slackened pace to circle more deliberately above the valley, all eyes on the eager watch for either Bruno or something to hint at his fate, Professor Featherwit lost a portion of that conviction.

If Bruno had indeed fallen victim to misplaced confidence, and had been craftily lured into this den of ravening wild beasts, why all this confusion and mad skurry? Why had not the traitor first made sure of his victim? Why such a general alarm?

Although such haste in getting afloat had been made, some little time had been thus consumed, and, before the aerostat was fairly above the Lost City, Bruno and Ixtli had dropped by stages down the shadowed side of the Temple of the Sun God, to burrow underneath the ground as their surest method of eluding pursuit.

Only for that, the end might have been different, for, once

sighted, Gillespie would have been rescued by his friends, or those friends would surely have shared death with him.

And so it came to pass that, circle though they might, calling ears to supplement their eyes, swooping perilously low down in their fierce eagerness to sight their imperilled one, never a glimpse of the young man could they obtain, nor even a definite hint as to where next to look for him.

"Surely they cannot have captured Bruno, as yet?" huskily muttered uncle Phaeton, hungrily straining his eyes without reward. "If the poor boy had actually fallen into such evil hands, why such crazy confusion? Why - oh, why did I permit his coaxings to overpower my better judgment? Why did I send him into -"

The words stuck in his throat and refused to issue. Phaeton Featherwit just then felt himself little less than a cold-blooded assassin.

Mr. Edgecombe was but little less deeply stirred, although his feelings were more of a mixture. He grieved for Bruno, and would willingly risk his life in hopes of doing the young man a service, yet his gaze was drawn far more frequently towards yonder temple, on the top of which he had - surely he HAD caught sight of his wife, his daughter!

"Let me down and try to find him," he eagerly begged, as one might plead for a great boon. "I promise to save him if yet alive, and - let me try, professor; I beg of you, give me this chance to show my heartfelt gratitude."

But Professor Featherwit shook his head in negation.

"That would only add to our trouble, friend. Knowing nothing of the dialect, you would be wholly at a loss. And, looking so entirely different in every respect, how could you hope to pass inspection?"

"All seems so confused, that I might - surely it is worth trying."

"It would be suicidal, so say no more on that score," almost harshly spoke the usually mild-mannered aeronaut, sending his vessel upon another circuit, only with stern vigilance choking back the appealing shout to his lost nephew.

This time the aerostat was brought directly above the Temple of the Sun, where there appeared to be some unusual disturbance, a number of armed guards fairly driving a gaily arrayed Indian down to the lower levels, and that greatly against his inclinations, judging from the harsh cries and ringing threats which burst from his lips.

Recognising the building, and unable to hold his intense emotions longer under stern control, Cooper Edgecombe called aloud the names of his wife and daughter, begging that they might come to him; but then the air-ship was sent onward and upward, with a dizzying swoop, and Professor Featherwit gripped an arm, sternly speaking:

"Quiet, sir! Another outbreak like that and I'll lock your lips, if I have to send a bullet through your mad brain!"

"I forgot. I could not wait longer, knowing that my loved ones -"

"You forgot that the lives of all depend upon our remaining at liberty," coldly interrupted Featherwit. "Without this means of conveyance, how can your loved ones escape? Now, your solemn pledge to maintain utter silence, or I will take you back to yonder wilderness, leaving you to shift for yourself as best you can. Promise, sir!"

"I will, - I do. Forgive me, for I was carried away by - 'twas there I saw - after so many horrible years!" huskily muttered the exile, fairly cowering there, before his saviour from the whirlpool.

"Enough; bear in mind that the rescue of your loved ones depend on our efforts. If discovered by yonder snarling beasts, and the machine is injured, - farewell, all hopes! Now, quiet, and look for Bruno!"

Again the air-ship circled over the valley, in spite of the moonlight passing wholly unseen and unsuspected by the Aztecs, whose energies were bent on ferreting out mortal foes, not demons of the upper world.

Waldo leaned farther over the hand-rail as they floated closer to an excited group of warriors, the central figure being Lord Hua himself, fiercely denouncing Aztotl and his son, Ixtli, as traitors to the common welfare, and calling upon all honest braves to mete forth befitting punishment.

Professor Featherwit caught one name indistinctly; that of the young Aztec in whose company Bruno had set forth on his ill-starred venture; and hoping to learn more of importance, he caused the aerostat to hover directly above that particular group of redskins.

Waldo, never stopping to count the risk he might thus fetch upon them all, silently lowered the grapnel, by means of the drag-rope, giving a boyish chuckle as the three-pronged hook descended amidst that gathering, the sight causing more than one superstitious brave to leap aside, with cries of amazed affright.

The air-ship gave a sudden swoop, and the grapnel caught Huatzin by his girdle, jerking him fairly off his feet, and swinging him into air, pretty much as a youngster might land a writhing fish. But no fish ever sent forth so wild a screech of mingled rage and terror as split the air just then.

Although hardly realising what was happening, Professor Featherwit sent the aeromotor upward with a mighty jerk. The shock proving too much for that sash, Lord Hua fell back to earth, literally biting the dust, although he met with no bodily harm beyond sundry bruises.

"Caught a sucker, and - I'll never do it again, uncle!" exploded Waldo, as he swiftly hauled in his novel fish-line; but he had to take a severe lecture from the professor before the subject was finally dropped.

And, worse than all else, the air-demon was now the target for both eyes and arrows, and, perforce, sailed swiftly away into the night.

CHAPTER XXVI.

DOWN AMONG THE DEAD.

Ixtli spoke with a degree of earnestness which left no room for doubt, even if the young man's own keen sense of hearing had not given warning but an instant later.

Ominous sounds came from the entrance, which had served them but so brief a time gone by, and Bruno knew that, even if they had escaped being seen while thus attempting to win such a gruesome refuge, the possibility of their having elected just such a line of flight had occurred to some of the redskins.

Gillespie heard the heavy doors open, then clang to again. He was fairly confident that some of the Aztecs had entered, although as yet the utter darkness hindered further recognition.

"What next, Ixtli?" he whispered, lips almost touching the face of his young guide, as they stood close together in the mirk. "They can't take me alive! Is it fight, or -"

"No fight yet," gently breathed the Aztec in turn. "Dey look, dat not make sure find. Dey try see; we try not see all time. Dey come, we go, - like dis!"

Catching a hand within his own clasp, Ixtli led Bruno away in that utter darkness, seemingly well acquainted with the lay of the ground, although it quickly became evident that there

JOSEPH E. BADGER, JR.

must be more than one direct passage. Bruno felt convinced that there were other chambers turning at right angles to their present course, though it might have bothered the young man to give entirely satisfactory reasons for such belief.

Ixtli did not flee fast nor far, in that first spurt, pausing shortly to turn face towards the rear, a low, musical chuckle coming through his lips.

"Dey come look, got no eyes for see in dark," he explained, barely loud enough for Bruno to catch his meaning. "We play fool dem all; dat be fun; heap fun all time over!"

Ixtli was scarcely as precise of speech while under the influence of excitement as when he had ample time in which to pick and choose his words; but there was little room for mistaking his meaning, which, after all, is fairly sufficient.

But this time the young brave was in error, for only a few moments later both fugitives caught sight of a dim light in hurried motion far towards the entrance to these underground crypts. That warned them of added peril, and Ixtli's chuckle died abruptly away.

"They'll fetch us now," grimly muttered Bruno, shaking his fairly athletic shoulders and fingering the knife at his belt as though making preparations for an inevitable struggle. "All right. They may kill, but I'll furnish some red paint for my tombstone, anyway!"

It may be doubted whether Ixtli fully appreciated this conclusion, yet he divined something of what was spoken, and made swift response:

"No kill yet. Dey look, we hide. Mebbe not find. Mebbe play fool all over - yes!"

"Where can we hide that lights won't ferret us out, though? If a fellow might only have the same advantage; here in this darkness I'm not worth a sick kitten!"

Just a bit disgustedly came the words, but Bruno was not giving over in weak despair. No matter how vast the odds might show against him, he would put up a gallant fight as long as he could lift his hand or strike a blow.

Still, he was by no means anxious for the crisis to arrive. He would far rather run than fight, under existing circumstances; but whither, and how?

Ixtli took it upon himself to solve the perplexing enigma, in a whisper bidding his white brother follow with as little sound as might be, once more hurrying away through the gloomy blackness, which was by no means rendered more agreeable to Bruno by that fleeting glimpse of the dead men's bones.

There was little room left for doubting the truth. Their presence in the death-cells surely was more than suspected, judging from the actions of yonder redskins, who flashed the light over and into each angle and corner, each niche and jog, where a human being might possibly seek concealment.

They were not so many in number, but still a larger force than could well be met with success by two youths, even granting that Ixtli would turn lethal weapons against his own people, which Bruno felt was by no means a settled fact.

For some little time the young men kept without that limited circle of light, watching each movement made by the searchers, and at the same time taking care that none of the little party stole a dangerous march upon them by hastening in advance of the lights.

Ixtli apparently enjoyed the affair, much as a child might a successful game of I-spy, for he emitted occasional chuckles, and let fall soft whispers which, if caught by other ears, certainly would not have deeply benefited the fugitives when captured.

Thanks to that slow progress, rendered thus by the care and minuteness of the search, Bruno began to marvel at the extent of the catacombs, and almost involuntarily calculate how many centuries it must have taken to accumulate such enormous quantities of remains. For, thanks to yonder prying light, he could see how high those grim relics of perishing mortality were piled up in tiers, with here and there upright skeletons in position of greater prominence.

Perhaps Gillespie might have been better able to appreciate Ixtli's amusement had he even an inkling as to how this game of hide-and-go-seek was fated to end. That an end must come, eventually, was a foregone conclusion. And then?

He ventured to ask Ixtli how they were to escape detection when they could retreat no farther, but before an answer could be fairly shaped, that end seemed actually upon them.

Without sound or warning of any sort, another bright light showed at a considerable distance in the opposite direction, and, as Bruno stared that way, he made out several armed warriors who appeared to be engaged in that same occupation: searching that city of the dead for the living!

Thus caught between two fires, there seemed only one course to pursue, and, with the courage of his fathers, Bruno spoke in low, grim tones to his young guide:

"No use for you to join in the mix, Ixtli. I'll do the best I know how, but if I can't make the riffle, if I go down for good and all, I ask you to convey the news to my friends. You will?"

But Ixtli was not at the end of his resources, and gripping a wrist, he urged Bruno towards yonder second light, speaking hastily as they moved along towards the edge of that wide passage. No fight, yet. Best hide; mebbe no find; dat best try first. Den Ixtli fight like white brother, - fast!"

There was time for scant speech, for just then the two parties seemed, for the first time, to catch sight of each other, and while the brave bearing the rude lantern still maintained his slow movements, searching well as he came, the other Indians came in advance, giving the fugitives barely time in which to crouch down under temporary cover.

The moment these enemies had passed them by, Ixtli urged Bruno on, then, in swift whispers, instructed him how to perfect his hiding, even aiding the young paleface into one of the upright crypts, back of a grim skeleton, the mouldering blankets assisting in covering the one of flesh and blood.

After like fashion, the Aztec sought cover on the opposite side of the passage. None too quickly, either; for now the single searcher drew dangerously nigh, peering into every practicable hiding-place on either side, before moving onward.

Little by little he drew closer, while the other band of searchers apparently turned off into a side passage, or large chamber, since nothing could be seen or heard of them by the fugitives.

In all probability, Ixtli's bold ruse would have proved a complete success, for the Aztec warrior showed no suspicion as he drew nearer; but it was not to be thus.

Fairly holding his breath, lest he disturb some of the dry bones immediately in front of himself, Bruno waited and hoped, only to feel his blood chill, and his heart fail him, as a sickening horror crept over his brain; nor was that the only creeping thing, - worse luck!

Past all room for doubting, his entrance into that crypt had disturbed the repose of a snake of some description; for now he could feel the loathsome reptile crawling slowly up his back, turning the skin beneath to scorching ice in its horrid passage.

One horrible nightmare minute that lasted, then the serpent paused upon his shoulder and biceps, touching his cheek with nose, then drawing back its ugly head to give an ominous hiss.

Human flesh and blood could endure no more, and Bruno flung the snake violently off, striking forcibly against that mass of dry bones as he did so. With a rattling clatter, the skeleton lost its frail coherence and tumbled outward, leaving Bruno fairly exposed within the niche.

With a cry the Aztec warrior turned in that direction, but ere he could fetch his light to bear upon the right spot, Ixtli sprung forth to the rescue, hooting like a frightened owl, as he dashed the light to earth, and, at the same time, deftly tripping the Indian headlong.

Swift as thought itself he followed up the advantage thus won, smiting the fallen brave heavily upon the crown with a clubbed thighbone, depriving him of sensibility for the time being at least. And then snatching up the still burning light, he called, in guarded tones, to his white friend:

"Come, brother, play hunt, now! Fast - not stop here; dat bad for you see by dem so soon. Dat good you go - like dis way!"

Scarcely realising just what fresh ruse the Aztec had in mind, but far from recovered from that horrible fear of death from poisonous fangs, Gillespie submitted, Ixtli hurrying him away, turning off into what appeared to be a side passage, less spacious than that to which they had until then confined their retreat.

The young Aztec hastily explained his present scheme, which was to play the role of searchers as well; and scarcely had he made that project known, than another difficult test was offered their courage.

CHAPTER XXVII.

PENETRATING GRIM SECRETS.

Bruno caught an imperfect view of moving figures at no great distance ahead, but ere he could fairly decide just what they might be, his red-skinned guide swiftly whispered:

"More come look. You don't say. Ixtli fool 'em - easy!"

Making not the slightest attempt to avoid the issue, the young Aztec stepped a little in advance of Gillespie, thus casting him into partial eclipse, speaking briskly, as he met the two Indians, only one of whom bore a light:

"It is trouble for nothing, brothers. There is no sign here. If he saw aught, 'twas in a dream, I think. And now - hark!"

Even there in the subterranean recesses something of the wildly excited uproar which followed Waldo's rash attempt to go a-fishing after his fellow men, and the sighting of that awful air-demon by the Indians, could be heard, and, without divining its actual import, Ixtli adroitly turned it to his own advantage.

"They have found the strange dog without!" he cried, sharply. "Come, my brothers, else we will be too late for - hasten, all!"

But only one-half of the present group obeyed, the two Indians dashing at full speed towards the main entrance to the city of the dead, leaving Bruno behind, wholly unsuspected, and Ixtli chuckling gleefully over the favourable change in the situation.

"Dey go - we come. Dis way, brother," the Aztec spoke, moving in the opposite direction, followed willingly enough by the now pretty well bewildered paleface.

"Whither are we going?" Bruno felt impelled to ask, after a few moments more of blind obedience. "How are we going to get out? And my friends, - they must have been alarmed by that great drum!"

Ixtli made response by touch rather than in words, and, giving his companion barely time sufficient to read aright that look of warning, he extinguished the light, leaving themselves in complete darkness.

Naturally anticipating fresh danger, Bruno strained his ears to catch at least an inkling of its precise nature ere the trouble could fairly close in; but only silence surrounded them, - silence, and an almost palpable gloom.

"Not cat," assured Ixtli, in a soft-toned whisper, as he divined the expectations entertained by his comrade in peril. "Nobody come, now. All gone see what noise 'bout, yonder. You, me, all right. Best mek no big talk, dough. Come - see!"

Apparently the young Aztec found it no easy matter to elect words which should fairly convey his desired meaning, and, abruptly giving over the effort, he moved on, one hand lightly closed upon Bruno's wrist to guard against possible separation in that utter darkness.

Nothing further was said until Ixtli again came to a halt, Gillespie giving a low exclamation as he felt what appeared to be a blank wall before them. Was this no thoroughfare? Were they blocked in, to perish of starvation, unless earlier discovered by the red-skinned searchers?

Far from agreeable thoughts, yet such swiftly flashed across the young man's brain, lending an echo of harshness to his voice as he spoke.

"Where are we now, Ixtli? How are we going to get out of this? If you have led me into a trap -"

Finger-tips lightly brushed his lips, then the Aztec explained as well he was able, thanks to his limited vocabulary.

Escape from the catacomb by the same route they had taken in seeking refuge there was entirely out of the question. Even though the redskins might have abandoned the search in that precise quarter for the time being, thanks to the sudden alarm which had broken forth in the valley, almost certainly there would be an armed guard so stationed as to intercept any or all persons who might so attempt to emerge.

This much Bruno gathered, then took his turn at the verbal oars.

"But we can't stay here, man, dear. Nothing to eat or to drink, and my friends worrying over us, outside. We've got to get out; I have, at any rate. The only question is, just how, and where?"

"Dere one way go," Ixtli made reply, even his lowered tones betraying more than ordinary impressiveness, Bruno fancied. "Mebbe easy, mebbe hard. Find dat, when try. We go dis way. Best be still, dough!"

Bruno was ready enough to promise all that, just so action was being taken, his uneasiness being by far too deep for rest or repose. More on account of his uncle and his brother, though, than for his own safety. He had not yet lost hope of extrication from the perils which surely surrounded them, not quite abandoned hope of rescuing the Children of the Sun as well.

Turning abruptly to the left, Ixtli led the way into what appeared (through the senses of touch and hearing) to be a

JOSEPH E. BADGER, JR.

narrow, winding tunnel, which presently took an upward incline, then broadened into a chamber of greater or lesser dimensions; the faint echoes told Gillespie there was an enlargement of some description, but the utter darkness veiled all else.

Barely had the two adventurous youths come to a pause, than dull, uncertain sounds came from almost directly above their heads; and, after listening for a brief space, Ixtli disappointedly breathed a fear that they would have to wait for the time being.

"Why? What's going on up yonder? And where are we, anyway?"

Beneath the great teocalli, Ixtli made answer in his disjointed way of speaking. There the evil-minded paba, Tlacopa, reigned supreme. And there, almost directly above their heads, stood the sacrificial stone, upon whose flat surface the Sun Children would be doomed to suffer the last penalty, provided Tlacopa won his wicked will.

Bruno thrilled to his centre with fierce indignation as he, little by little, gathered this information. Perish by such hideous methods? Give up her fair young life -

For, rather queerly, considering that Ixtli spoke of both Victo and Glady, he now had thought of - could see but that one lovely face and shrinking figure, - face and form of the daughter alone.

Discovery might have come all too soon, but for Ixtli's slipping a palm over those indignant lips and thus smothering the outbreak which the young man could not avoid; then, recalled to ordinary prudence, Bruno talked and listened by turns.

Ixtli contrived to make his white brother understand just how they were situated at the time: in a secret channel of communication with the great war temple, through which sanctuary he had hoped to lead his friend, thence to escape from the valley itself, if a favourable chance should offer. Now their way was barred, and they could only wait. Unless - would Bruno keep close guard over his tongue?

Yes. Anything, rather than remain wholly idle, like this.

Adding a few minor cautions, Ixtli took Gillespie by a wrist, and stole noiselessly forward, climbing upward, over and into a contrivance which Bruno vainly sought to recognise by the sense of touch, but giving a thrill of amazement when his guide paused long enough to whisper in his nearest ear:

"Dis war-god body. Stand up in teocalli, look on kill-stone. Wait; you see, hear, all dat, now!"

Thanks to the close association of that night, with all its attendant perils, Bruno was growing fairly skilful in interpreting the broken sentences of his copper-hued chum, and he now knew they were moving about within the hollow image of the Aztecan war-god, Huitzilopochtli, while -

He caught sight of several small apertures, through which yellow light came dimly, and, almost without thinking, applied his eyes to the one most convenient, peering forth upon the broad sacrificial stone, with its foul, blood-stained surface, the little channels intended to drain off the superfluous hemorrhage, together with the gloomy, repulsive surroundings. And, too, a most abominable stench appeared to rise from the altar of death, and Bruno shrunk back with a shiver of disgust.

"No talk loud!" softly breathed Ixtli, gripping an arm with force. "Dey kill, if find now. Look, dat one Tlacopa; big priest, you call. DEM help paba fool all people; so!"

Although his meaning was not fully apparent, Bruno caught renewed interest, and once more peered forth upon the scene, weird and impressive enough, even from a Christian point of view.

Headed by Tlacopa, a ceremony of some description was taking place, lesser priests and other acolytes performing their various parts, the incantations rising now loudly, now sinking to a hollow monotone, the whole affair being none the less absorbing when Bruno remembered that, perhaps, it might have some connection with the vile plots against the Sun Children, if not endangering life itself.

Gillespie likewise took note of various other graven images; among them one of the not less hideous war-goddess, Teoyaomiqui, or "divine war death," fitting consort for the mighty "humming-bird" himself.

Meanwhile, Ixtli, who appeared to look upon the whole affair as a more or less jolly good jest at the expense of his superstitious people, took occasion to give his white brother a few pointers, letting him see how easy it was for false oracles to be manufactured to order; how certain the lightest wishes of the head priest were to find speedy fulfilment at all times.

While thus divulging part of the mysteries of the temple, that ceremony reached a finale, and the little crowd slowly melted away, leaving but Tlacopa and a select few of his trusted henchman. And Ixtli certainly caught enough of their talk to alter his manner most materially.

"Come, quick!" he fiercely whispered in Bruno's ear, gripping an arm, and fairly forcing the young man to accompany his retreat.

Not another word was spoken before the lower level was reached, and then Gillespie broke the ice, asking what was the matter.

Dark though it was all around them, Bruno could tell by sense of touch that his guide was powerfully agitated, and, though Ixtli clearly hesitated before imparting the asked-for information, persistence won the point; and then -

Imperfectly though that discovery was set forth, Gillespie contrived to gather this much: Tlacopa decreed that the Sun Children should be brought to trial, if not to actual execution, when the morning sun arose!

"Never!" fiercely vowed Bruno, all on fire, as he recalled that more than fair face. "Never, - while I live and draw breath!"

CHAPTER XXVIII.

BROUGHT BEFORE THE GODS.

Once again Aztotl, the Red Heron, was bowing humbly before the Children of the Sun God, but now there was stern grief impressed upon his visage, rather than pure devotion, such as one might feel at the feet of a divinity.

And the face of Victo was unusually pale, her lips tightly compressed to keep them from trembling too visibly, while her arm clasped Gladys with almost fierce love in its warm strength.

Aztotl glanced upwards for a moment, then slowly spoke:

"Such are the commands laid upon thy captain of guards, Daughter of Quetzal', the Fair God. He hath been commanded to fetch Victo and Glady to the teocalli, there to be - no!" with an outbreak of fierce rebellion, drawing his superb figure erect, and gripping javelin until the springy ash quivered, as though suddenly winning life for itself. "The gods lie! They are speaking falsely, or - or the paba lies, when trying to thus interpret the oracle!"

Gladys shrunk away, but her mother stood firm, seeming to gain in coolness and nerve what this ardent servant was losing.

"It must be thus, my good friend," she spoke, in low, even tones. "The word hath come to a soldier, and obedience is his first duty."

"Not when obedience means leading to sacrifice -"

"That may never come, good Aztotl. We have committed no sin, in deed or in thought. The Mother of Gods will not lay claim to an innocent victim. Or, even then, the right shall triumph! Tlacopa is powerful, but hath Victo no influence? Lord Hua may throw HIS influence to the wrong side, but hath truth no answer?"

"If not truth, then death!" sternly vowed the captain of the body-guard. "If Tonatiuh fails to punish the enemies of his daughter, then this right arm shall hurl the false prince down to Mictlanteuctli, grim lord of the under-world!"

"What is it all about, mother?" murmured Gladys, clinging in sore affright to the side of her Amazonian relative. "Surely the people will not - surely we need not go forth to -"

A mother's kiss closed those quivering lips, and then, with far more assurance than she really could find in her heart, Victoria bade her child fear nothing; that all would come aright in a brief while.

Little by little, the maiden's terrors were calmed, and then she took position by her parent's side with a greater display of nerve than might have been anticipated.

Through all, Aztotl waited, fiercely silent, held from open rebellion only by the influence of the woman whose very life was now menaced. And as the Sun Children stood before him, in readiness to comply with the commands issued by those in high authority, the Red Heron broke bonds.

"Say but one word, Daughter of Quetzal', and all this shall never come to pass! Give me but permission to -"

"What wouldst thou do, good Aztotl?"

"Surround the Sun Children with their loyal body-guard and defend them, while one brave might strike blow, or hold shield in front of their sacred charge," slowly yet fiercely declared the captain, eyes telling how dearly he longed to receive that permission.

But Victo shook her head in slow negation. She was still cool of brain enough to realise how fatal such course would be in the end. If one deadly blow should be dealt, the end could be but one, - annihilation to both defended and defenders.

Then, too, she recalled the wondrous tidings brought the evening before by Ixtli and his comrade. Friends were seeking to rescue them, and if only time might be won - it must be played for, then!

And so, his petition finally denied, with no other course left open to take, the Red Heron summoned his picked band and, with the Sun Children in their midst, left the temple, crossed the plain, and slowly marched into the War God's teocalli.

In awed silence a vast number of Aztecs followed that little procession, silent as they, yet clearly anticipating events of far more than ordinary importance. And thus the foredoomed women were taken before the great stone of sacrifice, where-upon lay a snow-white lamb, bound past the possibility of struggling.

Close beside the prepared sacrifice stood the head priest, Tlacopa, robed for the awesome ceremony, sacrificial knife in hand, temples crowned as customs dictated, eyes blazing as vividly as they might if backed by living fire.

Not far distant stood Huatzin, head bandaged and face none the better looking for his floundering fall when his sash gave way the evening before. And as he caught the passing gaze of the woman whom he had so basely persecuted, a repulsive smile showed itself, the grin of a veritable fiend in human guise.

Sternly cold, and outwardly unmoved, the captain of guards performed his sworn duty, then in grim silence awaited the end. And in like manner each man of that carefully selected band rested upon his arms.

A brief pause, during which the utter silence grew actually oppressive, then the head priest lifted a hand as though commanding full attention before he should speak.

Then, in tones which were by no means loud, yet which were modulated so as to fill that expanse most perfectly, Tlacopa recited the grave accusations brought against the false children of the mighty Sun God.

To their evil influence he attributed the comparative failure of crops which had now cursed their fair people throughout the past years. Unto them, he claimed, belonged the evil credit of many untimely deaths which had covered so many proud heads with the ashes of mourning and of despair. To their door might be traced all of misfortune with which the favourite children of the mighty gods had been so sorely afflicted.

In proud silence Victo listened to this deliberate arraignment, not deigning to interpose denial, or offer plea in self-defence, until the paba was clearly at an end. And even then she gazed upon Tlacopa with eyes of scorn, and lips which curled with contempt.

A low murmur from the eager crowd told how anxious they were to hear more, and, taking her cue from that, Victo made a graceful motion with her white hand, following it by words that sounded rarely sweet in their deep mellowness, after the harsh, dry notes of the paba.

"Who dares to bring such base charges against the Daughters of Quetzal'? Who are our accusers, head priest?"

Did Tlacopa shrink from that queenly presence? If so, 'twas

but another cunning device intended to pave the way to complete success; to catch the fickle fancy of his audience by rendering his retort all the more effective.

"Who dares accuse us of wrong-doing?" again demanded the Amazonian mother, speaking for her child as well, around whose waist her left arm was clinging as a needed support.

"The Mother of all the gods!" forcibly replied the priest, now casting aside all presence of timidity, and gazing into that proud face with eyes which were filled with fire of hatred and jealousy. "The all-powerful Centeotl hath made known the awful truth through the lips of the infallible oracle, my children! She hath declared that no smiles shall be turned towards the children of Anahuac so long as false prophets disgrace this great city! She hath demanded the sacrifice -"

"Who can bear witness to any such demand?" sternly interposed the captain of the body-guard, unable to listen longer in silence.

Tlacopa flashed an evil look his way, but from the audience issued another murmur, rising louder until it took upon itself the shape of words, demanding indubitable proof that the oracle had indeed spoken thus. And, no longer daring to rely upon his own authority, Tlacopa turned to the sacrificial stone whereupon lay the helpless lamb, bowing knee and lifting face as he volubly repeated the customary invocation; just then it appeared far more nearly an incantation.

Having thus complied with all the requirements of his office, the paba first kissed his blade of sacrifice, then seized the lamb and turned it upon its back, one hand holding it helpless while with the other he ripped the poor beast wide from throat to tail, then, making a swift cross-slash, laid bare the cavity and exposed the quivering heart.

Dropping his knife, Tlacopa grasped this vital organ, fiercely tearing it away, drawing back where all might see as be lifted the heart on high for inspection.

One brief look appeared to satisfy his needs, for he gave a fierce shout as he hurled the bleeding heart towards the accused, then cried:

"An omen! An omen! The Mother of the Gods claims her victims!"

CHAPTER XXIX.

BENEATH THE SACRIFICIAL STONE.

Contrary to the expectations of Ixtli escape by way of the War God's temple was barred throughout the remainder of that eventful night. Tlacopa, the head priest, together with a number of his acolytes, varying as to force, yet ever too powerful for any two men to force a passage contrary to the will of their leader, remained on duty each and every hour. And hence it came to pass that those early hours found our fugitives still beneath the temple, worn through loss of sleep and stress of anxiety, yet firmly resolved not to permit that intended outrage without at least striking one fair blow for the Children of the Sun.

Slowly enough the time passed, yet it could hardly be called monotonous. Whenever wearied of their darksome waiting, the young men would steal again into the hollow image of Huitzil', there to utilise the cunningly arranged peepholes, now looking out upon the priests, or listening to catch such words as fell from the lips of those nearest the stone of sacrifice.

In this manner Ixtli contrived to pick up quite a little fund of information, mainly through the confidences reposed in a certain favoured few of the brotherhood by the chief paba. And this, in turn, filtered through his lips after the chums once again retreated to the lower regions for both safety and comfort.

And then Bruno learned how the adventurous young Aztec, far less superstitious than the vast majority of his people, thanks to the kindly teaching of Victo, Child of Quetzal', had in his explorations discovered so many secrets of the temple and priesthood, secrets which he now had no scruple in communicating to another of a different race.

Ixtli told how, on various occasions, he had lurked behind the scenes while the miraculous "oracle" was delivering fiat or prophecy, and then he told his white brother how Tlacopa meant to completely confound the Children of the Sun when once brought before the gods.

"He tell slave what say. Slave come dis way. Hide in War God. Wait for time, den tell Tlacopa's words!"

A most infernal scheme, yet the danger of which Bruno could readily recognise, together with the serious difficulty of refuting any such supernatural evidence.

"Surely your people will not suffer a few dirty curs to do such horrible wrong to ladies like - Why, Ixtli, even the gods you fellows bow the knee to in worship, ought to rise up in their defence!"

But Ixtli merely sighed, then spoke in sad tones, explaining how he alone had been taken wholly into the confidence of the Sun Children. Even the captain of their guards knew Victo and Glady as but descendants of the great Fair God whom the audacious trickery of a rival sent far away from the land of his favoured people, to find an abiding-place in the sun itself.

"He good brave. He die for dem, - easy! But he not know all. He think drop from sun, to lead people back to light. If think not so, dat make face turn black; dat make mad come - great big!"

As was ever the case when his feeling seemed deeply stirred, Ixtli found it difficult to fully or fairly explain his sentiments;

but Bruno caught sufficient of his meaning to give a fair guess at the rest.

He found a ray of hope in the belief that Aztotl at least would defend the Children of the Sun, and Ixtli predicted with apparent confidence that the members of the body-guard would stand firm under the Red Heron's leadership.

Keeping thus upon the alert throughout the remainder of that night, the young men were able to take prompt action when the crisis drew nigh.

Ixtli caught the first inkling of what was coming, and hastily sent Bruno away from the peepholes, dropping a word in his ear as they both prepared for clean work.

Through a secret entrance, shaped amidst the drapery which surrounded the pedestal of the mighty Huitzil', a slave of the temple crept to play the part of echo to Tlacopa's evil will; and scarcely had he secured what was to be a place of waiting and watching than the attack was made from out the darkness.

Ixtli flung his tunic over the slave's head, twisting both ends tightly about his throat, effectually smothering all attempt at crying aloud for aid, while Bruno clasped arms about his middle, holding hands powerless to strike or to draw weapon.

A brief struggle, which produced scarcely any noise, certainly not sufficient to reach the ears of priest or helper, then the trembling, unnerved slave was bundled down that narrow passage, to be dumped in a remote corner, and there effectually bound and gagged by the young men.

All this was performed without hitch or mishap, and then, nerved to fighting pitch, Ixtli and Bruno went back beneath the stone of sacrifice, resolved to play their part to the end in manful fashion.

There was no further fear of intrusion, for, of course, Tlacopa would never think of endangering his own evil scheme by risking an exposure such as would follow discovery of his slave-oracle. As Ixtli truly said, such discovery would end in the paba's being slain by his befooled people.

Their patience was sorely tried, even then, though a goodly portion of the blame belonged to their fears for the Sun Children, rather than to the actual length of waiting. But then, amidst the solemn invocations led by the high priest, the body-guard marched into the Hall of Sacrifice, and Bruno caught his breath sharply as he beheld - Gladys! Not her mother, just then. For the first minute, only, - Gladys!

Then came the bitter denunciation by Tlacopa, followed by the coldly dignified words of Victo, after which the innocent lamb yielded up its life in order that the future might be predicted through the still quivering heart.

With a fiercely exultant cry Tlacopa hurled the vital organ towards the accused, it striking the mother upon an arm, then glancing further to leave an ugly smear upon the daughter's shoulder ere falling among the eager multitude, who fought and struggled to secure at least a morsel of the hideous thing.

"Behold! the gods hath marked their own!" cried the high priest, his harsh tones fairly filling the Hall of Sacrifice. "They are guilty of all crimes laid at their door. They merit death, a thousandfold. The Mother of Gods hath spoken!"

"To whom but thou, Tlacopa?" sternly cried the captain of the guards, as he stood firm in spite of the ominous sounds which were rising from the rear, as well as from either side.

"She hath spoken unto me, as her worthy representative on earth."

"And there are those who say much religion hath turned thy brain, good Tlacopa," retorted Aztotl, holding his temper fairly well under control, yet with blazing eyes and stiffening sinews.

"Are thy ears alone to receive such important communications as -"

"Silence, thou scoffer!" fiercely cried the high priest, lifting quivering hands on high as though about to call down the thunders of an outraged deity upon that impious head. "She who hath spoken once may deign to speak again. Harken, - hear the oracle!"

Doubtless this was cue for the slave of the temple to repeat the words placed within its mouth, but that slave was literally unable to speak a word for himself, let alone others. Yet, - the oracle was not wholly silenced!

"Talk out, or I will!" fiercely muttered Bruno, giving Ixtli a violent punch in the side. "talk out for the Sun Children!"

The young Aztec needed no further prompting, loving Victo and Glady as he did, hating and despising the high priest. And in shrill, clear tones came the wondrous oracle:

"Tlacopa lies! Tlacopa is an evil dog! The Mother of the Gods loves and will defend her friends, the Children of the great and good Quetzal'."

How much more Ixtli might have said, had he been granted further grace, will never be known. Tlacopa shrank away from the speaking statue as from a living death, but then he rallied, savagely thundering:

" 'Tis a lying oracle! 'Tis an evil impostor who has - An omen! A true omen, my children! The evil ones hath been branded for the knife! Seize them! To the sacrifice!"

That vicious cry was swiftly taken up, but the body-guard closed in around the menaced women, presenting arms to all that maddened horde, while their captain sternly warned all good people to fall aside and make way for the Children of the Sun.

Then that secret entrance was flung wide, permitting two excited young men to issue, Tlacopa reeling aside from a blow dealt him by Bruno's clenched fist, as that worthy hastened to join forces with the body-guard.

CHAPTER XXX.

AGAINST OVERWHELMING ODDS.

This double appearance - for Ixtli kept fair pace with his hot-headed white brother - caused no little stir, and added considerable to the partial bewilderment which had fallen over that audience.

Prince Hua shouted forth savage threats, but he, as well as the paba, was fairly demoralised for the moment by the totally unexpected failure of their carefully laid schemes.

Seeing his chance, Aztotl bade his men escort the Sun Children from the Hall of Sacrifice back to their own abiding-place, barely noticing his son, and paying no heed at all to the disguised paleface.

With spears ready for stroke or parry as occasion might demand, the guard faced about and slowly moved away from the great stone of sacrifice, rigid of face, cool of nerve, ready to die if must be, yet never once thinking of disobedience to orders, or of playing cur to save life.

Almost involuntarily the crowd parted before that measured advance, giving way until a fair pathway lay open, along which the body-guard moved with neither haste nor hesitation, outwardly ignorant of the fact that ugly cries and dangerous gestures were coming thicker and faster their way.

Scores of other voices caught up the fierce cry given by the head priest, and now the temple was ringing throughout with demands that the false Sun Children should pay full penalty, should be haled to the sacrificial stone, there to purge themselves without further delay!

Others showed an inclination to favour the descendants of Quetzal', and thus the widely conflicting shouts and cries formed a medley which was fairly deafening.

For one of his fierce temper the Red Heron showed a marvellous coolness throughout that perilous retreat, and never more than during the first few seconds. Then a single injudicious word or too hasty movement might easily have precipitated a fight, where the vast audience would surely have brought disaster, whether the majority so willed or not.

Holding his men well in hand, moving only as rapidly as prudence justified, yet losing neither time nor ground, where both were of such vital importance; Aztotl forced a passage from the great Hall of Sacrifice down to the level, then out into the open air, where one could see and fight if needs be.

Through all this, Bruno Gillespie held the position he had taken, one hand gripping tightly his maquahuitl, but placing his main dependence upon the revolver which nestled conveniently within the folds of his sash, one nervous forefinger touching the curved trigger.

He could not help seeing that the danger was great. He felt certain that they could not retreat much farther without coming to blows, when the odds would be overwhelmingly against them. Yet never for an instant did he regret having taken such a decided step; not for one moment did he give thought to himself.

Almost within reach of his hand, if extended at the length of his arm, moved the fair maiden whose face and form had made so deep an impression upon his mind and his heart. She was in peril. She needed aid. That was enough!

Then the briefly stunned Tlacopa rushed forth from his desecrated temple, wildly flourishing his arms, furiously denouncing both the Sun Children and their body-guard, thundering forth the curses of all the gods upon the heads of those who refrained from arresting the evil ones.

"The mighty Mother of Gods calls for her own! Seize them! Strike down the impious dogs who dare attempt to defraud our Mother! Seize them! To the sacrifice - to the sacrifice!"

Equally loud of voice, the Prince Hua came leaping down to the sandy level, urging his people to the assault, offering almost fabulous sums as reward for the brave Aztec whose arm should lay yonder traitorous Red Heron prone in the dust.

The crisis came, and the dogs of war were let loose.

An arrow whizzed narrowly past the feathered helmet worn by the captain of the guards. A stone came humming out of sling, to be deftly dashed aside by Aztotl's shield ere it could fairly smite that gold-crowned head as, outwardly calm and composed, Victo aided her trembling daughter on towards the Temple of the Sun God, where alone they might look for safety.

But would it be found even there?

No! For, at savage howl from lips of the high priest, a strong force of armed redskins took up position at the teocalli, blocking each one of the four flights of stone steps in order to intercept the body-guard, while still closer pressed the yelling, screeching, frantic heathen of both sexes and all ages.

Aztotl saw how he had been flanked, but made no sign, even while slightly turning course for another temple at less distance, a single word being sufficient to post his true-hearts.

So far not a single blow had been struck by the retreating party, although great provocation had been given them. More than one of their number was bleeding, yet all were afoot, and still capable of holding ranks. Then -

Bravest of the brave, a man among men in spite of his tender years, Ixtli laid down his life in defence of his idolised Victo.

From one of that maddened rabble came a heavy stone, flung with all the power of a sinewy arm and great sling. Smitten fairly between the eyes, the poor lad's skull was crushed, as a giant hand might mash an eggshell.

One gasping sigh, then the lad sunk to earth, dead ere he could fairly measure his length thereupon.

For a single instant Aztotl seemed as one stupefied, but then an awful uproar burst from his labouring lungs, and he hurled his heavy javelin full at yonder murderer, winging it with a father's curses.

Swift flew the dart, but fully as quickly sank that varlet, the head of the spear scraping his skull, to pass on and smite with death one even more evil, if that might be.

Full in the throat Tlacopa was stricken, the broad blade of copper tearing a passage through, and the shaft following after for the greater portion of its length. Unable to scream, though his visage was hideously distorted by mingled fear and agony, the high priest caught the wood in both hands, even as he reeled to partly turn, then fall upon his face, dead, - thrice dead!

With a wild thrill of grief and horror, Bruno Gillespie saw his red brother reel in cruel death, and, for the moment heedless of his own peril, which surely was doubled thereby, he sprang that way, to stoop and catch that quivering shape in his eager hands.

Too late, save to show his comradeship. That heavy stone had only too surely performed its grim mission. Dead! Poor lad: dead, while seeking to save another!

With a fierce cry of angry mourning, Bruno lifted the mutilated corpse in his arms, trying to toss it over a shoulder, to bear away from risk of trampling under the heedless feet of the yelling heathen; but it was not to be. Another stone smote his arm near the elbow, breaking no bone, yet so benumbing the member as to temporarily disable it, causing that precious burden to drop to earth once more.

Then came an awful outcry from the people, whom the sight of their high-priest reeling in death had, for a few fleeting seconds, fairly stupefied. Cries which meant much to the living, and before which even that band of true-hearts receded with slightly quickened pace.

With the others fell back Bruno, leaving his hand-wood lying beside the lifeless corpse of his redskinned brother-at-heart,but drawing forth the weapon which he knew so much better how to use.

The fierce lust of vengeance now seized upon him, heart and brain. He shouted forth grim defiance to that howling crew, and as the deadly missiles came in thickening clouds, carrying death and wounds to the bodyguard of the Sun Children, he opened fire, shooting to kill.

Entirely without firearms themselves, and in all probability ignorant of such an instrument of destruction, this might have produced a far more beneficial result under other circumstances. As it was now, few, if any, took heed of what they could not hear above that awful tumult, and those who felt the boring lead never rose up to give their testimony.

Closer crowded the superstition-ridden heathen, showering missiles of all descriptions upon the body-guard, confounding all with the one to whose javelin their head priest owed his death, - only to recoil once more, in fierce awe, as another victim of high rank paid forfeit his life for the death of Ixtli, sole offspring of Aztotl, the Red Heron.

JOSEPH E. BADGER, JR.

CHAPTER XXXI.

DEFENDING THE SUN CHILDREN.

Louder than ever rose the voice of Lord Hua, after witnessing the fall of his ally, the high priest. In spite of the great odds against the body-guards, he began to fear lest his intended prey should even yet slip through his evil clutches.

Fiercer than ever rang forth his curses and imprecations upon the head of the Aztec who thus dared the vengeance of all the gods by lifting hand in arms against the anointed.

And then, his own nerve strung by those very efforts to inspire others, Lord Hua forged nearer the front, eager to behold all his hated enemies crushed to earth as by a single stroke. And then -

With vicious force he hurled his javelin straight for the white throat of the Sun Child who had scorned his fawning advances, and only the ever ready eye, the true hand, the strong arm of Aztotl again warded off grim death from the Fair God's Child.

Caught upon that trusty shield one instant, the next turned towards its original owner, to quiver for the barest fraction of time in that vengeful grip, then, gloriously true to the hero's will and intent, sped that javelin home.

Home to the false heart of false prince; grinding through skin and flesh and bones, cleaving that hot organ with broad blade of tempered copper, forcing one vicious screech from those tortured lungs, then causing that bulk to measure its length upon the blood-sprinkled sands.

Once again the heathen involuntarily recoiled, as death claimed a high victim. Once more the band of true-hearts slightly quickened their pace towards the temple, now nigh at hand. Yet those lessened numbers never once betrayed fear, or doubt, or faltering. Grimly true to their trust, they fell back in the best of order, fighting as they moved, beating back the heathen hosts, as though each man was a god, and their strong arms a wall of steel.

Here and there a true-heart sank to earth with the hand of death veiling his eyes, but he died in silence; no cry of fear, no moan of pain, no pitiful appeal for mercy at the hands of his maddened people. They knew their sworn duty, and like true hearts they trod that narrow path unto the very end.

Although with gradually lessening numbers, the body-guard remained practically the same. Still in a hollow square, with the Children of the Sun God in the centre, they slowly, doggedly fell back, ever facing the ravening foe, ever moving shoulder to shoulder as a single man.

Then, just as Bruno Gillespie was refilling his emptied revolver, the base of the tall pyramidal temple was won, and still protecting their fair-haired charge, the body-guard ascended to the second terrace, beating back such of the wild rabble as pressed them too closely.

Again that wonderful barking-death came into play, and Bruno felt a strangely savage joy gnawing at his heart as he saw more than one stalwart warrior reel dizzily back from his hot hail.

"For Ixtli, you curs! That for Ixtli! Down, - and eat dirt, dogs!"

Scarcely could his own ears catch those sounds, although he shouted with the full power of his strong young lungs, so indescribably horrid was the din and tumult.

Up another flight of steps, then yet another, although the crazed rabble was not pressing them so very hard, just now. Still, their number forbade a fourfold division as yet, and Aztotl feared lest the blood-ravening mob attempt to head off their flight by taking possession of the other stairs, thus being first to occupy yonder flat arena high above the earth, whereupon he hoped to still protect the Sun Children, even though he must lay down his life to maintain their lease.

Lacking an acknowledged leader, the furious mass thought only of crushing the faithful band by mere weight of numbers, taking no thought in advance, else the end might well have been precipitated.

Arrows, spears, javelins, stones from slings, poured upon the body-guard in almost countless numbers, now and then claiming a true-heart as victim, whereupon the rabble howled afresh in drunken triumph; but where a single man died in the performance of his oath-bound duty, half a score heathen bit the dust and grovelled out his remnant of life yonder where most viciously trampled the feet of his fellow brutes.

Pausing barely long enough to beat back the crazed rush which came so close upon their retreat, the band of brothers would then slowly, doggedly fall back another of those mighty steps, with bared teeth and blazing eyes, longing to end all by one joyous plunge into the thick of their assailants, dying with their chosen dead!

Five separate times that upward flight, and five times the grim pause to give death another portion of his red feast. Five times the blood-lapping mob dashed against the band of brothers. Five times they were hurled back, leaving more dead and dying there to mark the savage struggle.

And then, sadly decimated at each halt, less in numbers as they passed farther from earth to climb nearer the blue sky, the survivors won the crest of the teocalli, still fighting, still beating back such as followed their steps more closely.

Ere that brilliant retreat began, 'twould have taken close ranks for the body-guard to find standing-room upon the temple-top; but now - Aztotl called for a division of his force, since there were four separate avenues of approach, of which the enemy was prompt to avail itself.

"For the Sun Children, my brothers!" he cried, his voice rising even above that awful tumult and turmoil. "Guard them with your lives!"

Little need to waste breath in so adjuring. Of all thus enlisted, not one of the true-hearts but proved worthy the trust.

Not one brave who took care for his own life. Not one but was ready to die in order to save; and thus far not a single wound had won so far as either Child of the Fair God.

Even now while the heathen were raging more viciously than ever, crowding each terrace and jamming each flight of steps to the verge of suffocation, strong arms were shielding them, true hearts were thinking how best they might be served.

Time and again Aztotl warded away winged death as it sought to claim Victo for its prey. And Bruno Gillespie, no whit less brave if somewhat lacking in warlike experience, made Gladys his especial care, sending shot or dealing knife-thrust in her defence, barely giving thought to his own safety as a side issue.

Those broad terraces bore ugly pools and irregular patches of red blood. The various flights of stone steps grew slippery and uncertain as they likewise began to steam. Yet forward and upward pressed the howling mob, and desperately fought the doomed body-guard above.

Faster fly the deadly missiles, too many by far for even the keenest eye to guard against them all. One and another of those gallant defenders drop away; only because death had claimed them, not because of fear or of bodily anguish.

Aztotl staggers, - an arrow is quivering in his broad bosom, - but still he fights on, dealing death with each blow of his blood-dripping hand-wood. A stone lays open his brow, - but heavier and faster plays his terrible weapon. A javelin flashes briefly, then the red copper vanishes from sight, while the ashen shaft slowly dyes crimson, as the hot life-blood issues.

A last, dying stroke, and the Red Heron sinks at the feet of his adoration, faithful unto the last, his brave soul going forth to join with that of Ixtli; the last of a gallant family.

Victo gives a wild cry of vengeance, then snatches up bow and quiver where let fall by a death-smitten warrior, and wings swift death to the slayer of her captain of the guard.

An awful melee, where the odds were momentarily increasing; where one man was forced to do the work of a score; where death inevitable awaited all, unless a miracle should intervene. And that miracle -

Shrilly rang forth the voice of Victoria Edgecombe as, amidst the fury of battle, she caught sight of the air-ship swiftly darting that way through the clear atmosphere, bent on saving, if saving might be.

The peculiar sound which attended the exploding of a dynamite cartridge heralded the death of more than one Aztec, and, as the swift rattle of revolvers added to the uproar, there was an involuntary recoiling, a terrified shrinking, which was employed to the best advantage by the air-voyagers.

The aerostat barely landed upon the top of the temple, before Cooper Edgecombe, with a wild scream of ecstatic joy, caught his wife in his arms and hurried her into the car, while Waldo and uncle Phaeton aided Bruno.

CHAPTER XXXII.

ADIEU TO THE LOST CITY.

And Bruno clung fast to the half-swooning maiden, so that two in place of one had to be assisted by uncle and nephew!

Barely a score of seconds thus employed, then the gallant air-ship responded to the touch of master-hand, and floated away from the bloody temple-top with its increased burden, even as the last survivor of the Sun Children's body-guard sank down in death.

A brief stupor came over the amazed heathen at sight of this awful air-devil from whose sides spat forth invisible death; but then, as they divined at least a portion of the truth, as they saw their longed-for victims thus borne bodily away, a revulsion came, and, amid the most hideous howls and screeches, missiles flew towards the air-ship, menacing sudden death to all therein.

But fate would not have it thus, and, under the guidance of that master-hand, the aeromotor flew higher and farther, quickly leaving behind all peril from javelins, darts, arrows, or stones from slings. And but one of their number had suffered aught: Bruno lay as one dead, blood flowing from a stone-gash over an eye, but with one hand still gripping the butt of an empty pistol; his other arm was - around the Sun Daughter's waist!

And Gladys? First she shrunk back with a gasping cry of mingled fear and grief; only to quickly recover and - did she kiss that curiously spotted, streaked face?

Waldo afterwards declared she certainly did, for that a moment later he saw some of that moistened stain upon her quivering lips; but Waldo was ever extravagantly fond of a jest, and it may be - never mind!

Not until the air-ship was safely past peril from yonder howling, raving lunatics in bronze did Professor Featherwit give heed to aught else, and by that time Victoria had left the ardent embrace of her husband, to care for the elder Gillespie, whose single-hearted devotion all through that bloody retreat and bloodier struggle upon the temple had not wholly escaped her notice.

Under such tender ministrations, Bruno quickly revived, and, after assuring himself that the Children of the Sun were alive and unharmed, while the Lost City was now left far behind them, he huskily begged uncle Phaeton to descend to earth, where he might find water enough to remove what remained of that loathsome disguise!

But Professor Featherwit was far too shrewd a general to take any unnecessary risks. His last glimpse of yonder valley showed him hundreds of armed redskins rushing at top speed for the various passes by which that circle of hills could be over-passed, and he knew that chase would be made as long as the faintest ray of hope lured the Aztecs on.

Thus it came that no halt was made until the inland reservoir was reached, where there could be no possible danger in making a temporary landing. And then Bruno stole away in hot haste, both to wash his person and to reclothe it in garments not quite so ridiculous as he now felt that savage rig must appear.

"Just as though the little woman wasn't used to see fit-outs like that, old man," mocked Waldo, the irrepressible. "She'll go scare at you in this rig; see if she doesn't, now!"

Whether or no Gladys was actually frightened as Bruno made his appearance, need not be decided here; but one fact remains: she acted a vast deal shyer than when she saw her gallant defender lying as if dead, with the red blood flowing over his face.

Naturally enough, Cooper Edgecombe seemed fairly crazed by his joy. After so many long years of hopeless grief and wistful longing, to find his loved ones, safe and sound, far more beautiful than of yore! Surely enough to turn the gravest of men into a laughing, jesting, voluble lad!

But throughout it all ran a vein of sadness and of mourning. Neither Aztotl the noble, nor Ixtli the gallant, could so soon be forgotten. And more than one pair of eyes grew dim, more than one voice turned husky, as mention was made of both life and death, - peace to their ashes!

Heavily burdened as the air-ship now was, it would be unwise to add more, and so but a few minor articles were removed from the cavern, which had for so long sheltered the exiled aeronaut, then the lever was touched, and the vessel rose slowly into air, making one leisurely circuit of the lake, in order to show the Children of the Sun where their husband and father came so perilously nigh to entering upon a subterranean voyage to the far-away Pacific. And, luckily as it appeared, they were just in time to see that "big suck" drag another huge tree down into its ever hungry maw.

Not until the shades of night again began to settle over the earth did the professor permit another halt, but then many miles lay between that Lost City of the Aztecs and their present position, and, after selecting a pleasant spot for alighting, preparations for their first al-fresco meal in company were begun.

That proved to be a pleasant meal, and yet a more pleasant evening there in the wilderness, - the first, but by no means the last, partaken of, - for, now they need no longer fear the heathen, Professor Featherwit was eager to more thoroughly explore that strange land.

Still, the air-ship was inconveniently crowded, and that helped to cut explorations short. Then, too, Cooper Edgecombe was naturally eager to return to civilisation once more, especially as he now had his heart's dearest desire, wife and daughter, each peerless in her peculiar way.

Thus it came to pass that the terra incognita was abandoned for the time being, Professor Featherwit striking that wide path of ruin which marked the course of the tornado, then sailing leisurely towards the point of their initial departure, improving the opportunity by giving a neat little lecture concerning tornadoes in general, and that one in particular.

"Which totally exploded so many absurd theories held up to date," was his proud assertion; and then he went on to explain just how, and why, and wherefore -

Why dwell longer? The tale I set out to narrate is finished. The unknown land has been penetrated, and at least a portion of its marvels has been inspected; imperfectly, no doubt, but that may be attributed to circumstances which were past control.

And should the still curious reader ask, "Is it all true? Is there actually such a place as the Lost City? And are the people who live in that town really and truly the same race as once inhabited Old Mexico?" - to all such, I can hardly do better than this: there was a Territory of Washington. There is now a State of Washington. Within that State may be found a range, or system of mountains, known to the world as the Olympics. And within the wide scope of country which lies nestling inside of that mountain system may to this day be found -

But, after all, a little parable which Waldo Gillespie read to a certain doubting Thomas, on the very evening of the day which changed Gladys Edgecombe, spinster, into Mrs. Bruno Gillespie, may better serve in this connection.

"After all, I don't believe there is any such place or people," declared Doubting Thomas, nodding his head vigorously.

"Is that so?" mildly queried our good friend, Waldo. "Let me give you a little pointer, old man. Once upon a time, a man by the name of John Smith was being tried for stealing a fat hog. The State brought three reputable witnesses to swear that they actually saw the theft committed, while the best the defence could offer was to declare that they could produce at least a dozen honest citizens who would make oath to the fact that they did not witness the crime. So - moral:

"We six fairly honest people saw both the Lost City and its inhabitants. Scores of equally reliable persons never saw either. Which sort of evidence weighs the most, my good fellow?"

Gentlemen of the jury, the verdict rests with you!

Choose from Thousands of 1stWorldLibrary Classics By

Adolphus William Ward
Aesop
Agatha Christie
Alexander Aaronsohn
Alexander Kielland
Alexandre Dumas
Alfred Gatty
Alfred Ollivant
Alice Duer Miller
Alice Turner Curtis
Alice Dunbar
Ambrose Bierce
Amelia E. Barr
Andrew Lang
Andrew McFarland Davis
Anna Sewell
Annie Besant
Annie Hamilton Donnell
Annie Payson Call
Anton Chekhov
Arnold Bennett
Arthur Conan Doyle
Arthur Ransome
Atticus
B. M. Bower
Basil King
Bayard Taylor
Ben Macomber
Booth Tarkington
Bram Stoker
C. Collodi
C. E. Orr
C. M. Ingleby
Carolyn Wells
Catherine Parr Traill
Charles A. Eastman
Charles Dickens
Charles Dudley Warner
Charles Farrar Browne
Charles Ives
Charles Kingsley
Charles Lathrop Pack
Charles Whibley
Charles Willing Beale
Charlotte M. Braeme
Charlotte M.Yonge
Clair W. Hayes
Clarence Day Jr.
Clarence E. Mulford

Clemence Housman
Confucius
Cornelis DeWitt Wilcox
Cyril Burleigh
D. H. Lawrence
Daniel Defoe
David Garnett
Don Carlos Janes
Donald Keyhole
Dorothy Kilner
Dougan Clark
E. Nesbit
E.P.Roe
E. Phillips Oppenheim
Edgar Allan Poe
Edgar Rice Burroughs
Edith Wharton
Edward J. O'Biren
John Cournos
Edwin L. Arnold
Eleanor Atkins
Elizabeth Cleghorn
Gaskell
Elizabeth Von Arnim
Ellem Key
Emily Dickinson
Erasmus W. Jones
Ernie Howard Pie
Ethel Turner
Ethel Watts Mumford
Eugenie Foa
Eugene Wood
Evelyn Everett-Green
Everard Cotes
F. J. Cross
Federick Austin Ogg
Ferdinand Ossendowski
Francis Bacon
Francis Darwin
Frances Hodgson Burnett
Frank Gee Patchin
Frank Harris
Frank Jewett Mather
Frank L. Packard
Frederick Trevor Hill
Frederick Winslow Taylor
Friedrich Kerst
Friedrich Nietzsche
Fyodor Dostoyevsky

Gabrielle E. Jackson
Garrett P. Serviss
Gaston Leroux
George Ade
Geroge Bernard Shaw
George Ebers
George Eliot
George MacDonald
George Orwell
George Tucker
George W. Cable
George Wharton James
Gertrude Atherton
Grace E. King
Grant Allen
Guillermo A. Sherwell
Gulielma Zollinger
Gustav Flaubert
H. A. Cody
H. B. Irving
H. G. Wells
H. H. Munro
H. Irving Hancock
H. Rider Haggard
H. W. C. Davis
Hamilton Wright Mabie
Hans Christian Andersen
Harold Avery
Harold McGrath
Harriet Beecher Stowe
Harry Houidini
Helent Hunt Jackson
Helen Nicolay
Hendy David Thoreau
Henrik Ibsen
Henry Adams
Henry Ford
Henry Frost
Henry James
Henry Jones Ford
Henry Seton Merriman
Henry Wadsworth
Longfellow
Henry W Longfellow
Herbert A. Giles
Herbert N. Casson
Herman Hesse
Homer
Honore De Balzac

Horace Walpole
Horatio Alger, Jr.
Howard Pyle
Howard R. Garis
Hugh Lofting
Hugh Walpole
Humphry Ward
Ian Maclaren
Israel Abrahams
J.G.Austin
J. Henri Fabre
J. M. Barrie
J. Macdonald Oxley
J. S. Knowles
J. Storer Clouston
Jack London
Jacob Abbott
James Allen
James Lane Allen
James Andrews
James Baldwin
James DeMille
James Joyce
James Oliver Curwood
James Oppenheim
James Otis
Jane Austen
Jens Peter Jacobsen
Jerome K. Jerome
John Burroughs
John F. Kennedy
John Gay
John Glasworthy
John Habberton
John Joy Bell
John Milton
John Philip Sousa
Jonathan Swift
Joseph Carey
Joseph Conrad
Joseph Jacobs
Julian Hawthrone
Julies Vernes
Justin Huntly McCarthy
Kakuzo Okakura
Kenneth Grahame
Kate Langley Bosher
L. A. Abbot
L. T. Meade
L. Frank Baum
Laura Lee Hope

Laurence Housman
Leo Tolstoy
Leonid Andreyev
Lewis Carroll
Lilian Bell
Lloyd Osbourne
Louis Tracy
Louisa May Alcott
Lucy Fitch Perkins
Lucy Maud Montgomery
Lydia Miller Middleton
Lyndon Orr
M. H. Adams
Margaret E. Sangster
Margaret Vandercook
Maria Edgeworth
Maria Thompson Daviess
Mariano Azuela
Marion Polk Angellotti
Mark Overton
Mark Twain
Mary Austin
Mary Cole
Mary Rowlandson
Mary Wollstonecraft Shelley
Max Beerbohm
Myra Kelly
Nathaniel Hawthrone
O. F. Walton
Oscar Wilde
Owen Johnson
P.G.Wodehouse
Paul and Mable Thorn
Paul G. Tomlinson
Paul Severing
Peter B. Kyne
Plato
R. Derby Holmes
R. L. Stevenson
Rabindranath Tagore
Rahul Alvares
Ralph Waldo Emmerson
Rene Descartes
Rex E. Beach
Richard Harding Davis
Richard Jefferies
Robert Barr
Robert Frost
Robert Gordon Anderson
Robert L. Drake

Robert Lansing
Robert Michael Ballantyne
Robert W. Chambers
Rosa Nouchette Carey
Ross Kay
Rudyard Kipling
Samuel B. Allison
Samuel Hopkins Adams
Sarah Bernhardt
Selma Lagerlof
Sherwood Anderson
Sigmund Freud
Standish O'Grady
Stanley Weyman
Stella Benson
Stephen Crane
Stewart Edward White
Stijn Streuvels
Swami Abhedananda
Swami Parmananda
T. S. Ackland
The Princess Der Ling
Thomas A. Janvier
Thomas A Kempis
Thomas Anderton
Thomas Bailey Aldrich
Thomas Bulfinch
Thomas De Quincey
Thomas H. Huxley
Thomas Hardy
Thomas More
Thornton W. Burgess
U. S. Grant
Valentine Williams
Victor Appleton
Virginia Woolf
Walter Scott
Washington Irving
Wilbur Lawton
Wilkie Collins
Willa Cather
Willard F. Baker
William Makepeace Thackeray
William W. Walter
Winston Churchill
Yei Theodora Ozaki
Young E. Allison
Zane Grey